JAMES PARK SLOAN, who grew up in South Carolina and Chicago, is a Harvard graduate who served as a paratrooper in Vietnam. WAR GAMES, his first novel, won the New Writers Award for best novel of the year. The Prize Committee called it "a novel notable for its depiction of a frighteningly real world."

To
Jeanette Pasin Sloan
and
Mark Van Doren

☆ *part one* ☆

★ one ★

TODAY I WENT to the dentist. He asked if I would mind a temporary filling, only until a shipment of the preferred material arrives from the states. I said by all means.

He confirmed what I have learned about the dental bill of rights. When the army repairs a tooth, it is obligated to care for that tooth for the rest of your life. The adjacent ones as well. I have begun going to the dentist with regularity, complaining of pains in every third tooth. The teeth are marked on my chart by his technician, whom I pester continually. The dentist treats each one, and by the end of my tour the government is going to be legally responsible for my entire mouth.

Since my purpose here is blunted, I have been dwelling on trivia. My day-to-day life is very much an interim event. Perhaps that is about to change. Good luck with the dentist may be an omen.

So far I have been unlucky. My dream was to write a war novel. The definitive novel of Vietnam, it would be. I thought I might call it *A Small War*. In order to gather material I would disguise myself. I would pretend to be a soldier like everybody else. It wasn't

9

hard to disguise myself. I am only twenty. I left Harvard after my sophomore year.

It's not being easy to write the great war novel about Vietnam while stuck on garrison duty in Korea. I have good ideas all right, but I need filler. Colors, things people said, the way food tasted—details like that. Most of all I need to find out which of my two theories is the correct one.

THEORY ONE

The timid hero goes to Vietnam like a sissy dipping his toe in the pool. Suddenly he realizes that he can be a cold-water swimmer. This happens because Vietnam provides him with a character-molding experience. It is both purposeful and earthshaking. There is a flash of insight. He realizes that he is now fully mature. He has become a soldier and a man.

This is only a hypothesis. Then there is Theory Two.

THEORY TWO

A tough-minded young man, who unsuspectingly has above-average sensitivity, goes to Vietnam. For the first time in his life he encounters genuine brutality and tragedy—perhaps his first tragic love affair. This experience shocks him into his own humanity. There is a flash of insight. He comes home in total revulsion at war and probably writes a book.

There are also innumerable ancillary issues: whether the war is justified, whether war *period* is justified, who is going to win the war, and what victory or defeat will mean. Most of these questions are hard to answer, even when one has experience, but fortunately from the individual point of view they are not very important. It is important only to find out which model of the war novel applies and to write that novel with a maximum of local color from Vietnam.

In order to be prepared, should I ever get to Vietnam, I have been reading and rereading war novels. A *Farewell to Arms*, *All Quiet on the Western Front*, *The Red Badge of Courage*, they should train me to organize my experience into the proper form. After all, I can't expect my personal experiences to happen just like a novel. If I read enough, I can at least shape my life more like a story. At the same time I can be learning what kind of things to invent, for instance, if I have to die or be in some way incapacitated. Wars differ. Some wars are the kind that timid young men achieve manhood in, while others are the kind that make tough guys throw up everytime they think of it for ten or fifteen years. There is a good deal of talk about Vietnam, one way or the other. But so far there is nothing definitive.

If I can decide which type of book should be written about Vietnam, I'm sure my book will be the definitive one. For this reason, I think little details are important. Not only are they necessary as filler between the important scenes, but I will need all the data I can get when the time comes to decide how I am going to feel about the war. Even the events that preface my going to Vietnam may prove important. That's my purpose in setting things down beginning with my arrival in Korea.

It was the week of heavy rains. Roads and bridges were washed out. Refugees were brought onto the post, tagged, and crowded into vacant barracks. By chance the depot was less than half full. Some of the refugees even received sheets. Mechanized units took to the field on missions of mercy. Amphibious tracks were floated across the nearby river with evacuation-lift wire. The good will of the populace was bound to us with one more strap.

In the absence of electric power, dental drills were inoperable. Since that time, teeth have been on my

11

mind. The people and mountains never had a chance. In the mess hall at replacement depot a sucking pain attacked the left side of my head. I thought immediately of the powdered milk. It is reassembled in Seoul, in a huge vat that looks like a concrete mixer, but the troops are not deceived. So . . . a bad batch. But no; seconds passed. Local. Toothache. Molar! Drinking milk merely stimulated the nerve. Saliva did the same. Taste was not culpable at all. Still, I've never felt the same about reconstituted milk.

The flight to Korea had softened me up, left me without reserve. The stewardess had a good figure, but a repelling case of acne. Perhaps a group of soldiers had been polled and their preferences allowed for. Perhaps nothing mattered on this particular flight. It's the one going the other way that counts. That's the one that drums up the future business.

We flew west a step ahead of the sun. By the time we took off from a lengthy unexplained stopover in Seattle, we were hovering on top of dawn. For fourteen hours we rode her rosy back. Every hour or so the stewardess appeared with a tray of powdered eggs. There were also snacks, waffles, and mushy apples. The leadbelly stickrib stuff was cut with juice and a vigorously laxative coffee. Not a breakfast man myself, I called the stewardess to ask for a steak, a sandwich, anything to break out of the pattern. She refused with regrets, saying the situation couldn't be helped. If it's dawn, it's dawn, and the airline can't do a thing about it. I took a nap. The smell in the close quarters was overwhelming. At Tokyo, the cups of coffee were replaced by tea. The stewardess was replaced by an Oriental, her eyefold surgically adapted to widen the lotus-petal slit. Before we were out of sight of Tokyo, she appeared with a tray of powdered eggs. In retrospect, I place the first twinge at the time we began descending into Kimpo.

After three days of processing, of Darvon and restless, unwanted sleep, I was notified that someone had discovered an old mechanical drill put away for field operations. Waiting for the dentist to call me, I recalled having heard it mentioned about the army's dental obligations. I made a note to look it up in regulations and frame an appropriate policy.

Another malady was not so easily to be neutralized. My journey had stopped short of its destination. Dissatisfied with Korea, I contracted a sickness peculiar to the malcontent.

My training had taken place at Leonard Wood—mocked by the residents as "Little Korea." Returning veterans began the convention after the war. It is the work of a simple and vulgar mentality; I am sure that within a year or two the bases located in southern areas will be uniformly known as "Little Vietnams." The fact is that between wars we miss the ugliness and deprivation.

My fellows claim that Koreans are the ugliest folk that God saw fit to propagate. Subhumans, virtually. They claim the Korean Adam was hit across the facial plane with a shovel—pardon, an intrenching tool. The national profession is the slicky trade. Drive a truck through the center of Munsan, it is suggested, and see how much of the cargo remains after a half mile. Vehicles must carry an armed guard above the rear bumper. They call this the only land in the world where you can stand waist deep in mud and be pelted in the face with sand. Its summers are the hottest and wettest, its winters the most brutally cold (though on this score I am not deceived; I have heard them say the same of Germany). There is a superfluity of mountain, put there to tax the legs and increase the maintenance on vehicles. The countryside is bleak. The only

13

attractions are burial mounds, which must be avoided when one is driving a tank.

These deficiencies failed to capture my attention. For me, there was but one fault, the absence of a war. True, a satisfactory treaty had not been signed, but a resumption of hostilities seemed unlikely. An inadequate document says nothing for the state of conflict. Men stop fighting when they have had enough of it, and in this locale they have had enough. As far as they are concerned, the differences are settled by tacit compromise. Placidity has prevailed, a most unsatisfactory condition for contributing to my élan.

Meanwhile, *my* war, the war I discovered, is being stolen. It had been hidden in a pamphlet decrying our impositions on foreign lands, in this case a small country formerly part of Indochina. The others were skipping it as a bore on the innermost pages of the *Times*. It became *my* project, and I even learned the more recent spelling before it was used by the *Times*. A strong sense of propriety began to develop. But getting sent to a war takes time. The army has its notions, seniority for the most part. For a very long time, service was restricted by rank and special credentials. It was as if there were not enough to go around, and it had to be limited to those in need of the professional experience. Suddenly things have changed, and it is being parceled out to every Tom and Harry who isn't making it at college. Orders arrive unsought, and off they go, embittered. It is better that my jealousy not be expressed. The war is rightfully mine, but by tortuous administrative logic, I have to sit and watch it debased. I feel for it as for the great book in public libraries. Someone should have guarded it from democratic usage.

Thus the malady. No sooner had I arrived than I began to make plots. It is my firm intention to fight the war in my remaining months of service. I have no notion of reenlisting. The orderly flow of my life must not be interrupted. The war must take place in my spare time, so to speak, before getting down to serious business. Such is my concept of the military as a whole. It is an interlude required of every complete and cultivated man. Socrates himself served as a common soldier in a war the purpose and outcome of which are never mentioned. It is a part of liberal education.

My friend M. would be disturbed at these sentiments, particularly at the admission to laying plots. A hero does not make plots, he would tell me, but is noble in the face of them. Achilles would be cited, of the noble unpremediation, who slaughtered multitudes for an insult and a web of circumstances that others spun.

Poor M.! He sits in the Cook County Jail, the price of his spontaneity when he saw a policeman drag a woman by the hair. I must write and make clear my feeling that there were nothing wrong in what he did per se. It's only that he stumbled onto the scene without malice aforethought.

He did not emerge the hero, for heroes are inveterate plotters. Not by pure intentions came Odysseus, nor Quixote. The whole world is a counterplot to frustrate the epic mood! The hero must not merely thrash the villains, but create them. Set them up for the kill like the matador his bull. Lay hold to a portion of the banal, flog it to life, and from it fashion an adversary worthy of his steel. I shall remember to cite Hamlet: devise the play, then act in it!

★ two ★

My state of mind appeared impervious to detours. While in Korea, I intended to maintain an attitude of annoyance and resignation. No diversions, no ups and downs. I even brushed aside the toothache, thinking to show disdain for small matters.

From clerk to clerk I took my intention to move on with minimal inconvenience. Although I made vague offers, there were no takers. To the contrary, one of them brought me into his own confidence. He had made an error in channeling arrivals. Would I consent to a change of orders on his behalf? I had just finished a spiel on the necessity to stick together and circumvent regulations. Although we had not met before that hour, what could I say? For all I knew, he might have had the power to transfer me regardless. Perhaps if I played ball with him, someone in the future would play ball with me. I soon forgot the favor and proceeded to a different unit, thinking that if you are not where you wish, it may as well be one wrong place as another.

Mail call after mail call I watched the other soldiers pretending to smell perfume through the envelopes. The absence of mail never surprises me; it only annoys me that the chance of getting a letter forces me to stand in formation while the other names are called. I am a bad correspondent myself. Often a letter to M. will sit around for a month before I put it in an envelope, and perhaps another before I stamp it and drop it in a box.

I ignore the regulation requiring soldiers to put their return addresses on envelopes. I reason that the very act of omission protects the culprit. If an official opens a letter, he himself is in violation of a statute. Thus no return address; my friends know very well where I am.

In the beginning the absence of mail was natural. It almost never keeps up with one's own movements. Later I assumed airlift preempted; the buildup and all. Then there were the floods between here and Seoul. After a time I inquired from the other soldiers and found that their mail was arriving as usual.

My fiancée must be sick; or she had met with an accident. It worried me to think this; yet one assumes the minimal revision, leaving the larger structure whole. But would not her parents have written? Perhaps they were holding it from me.

To make it worse, I had mentioned my address in writing home and parental letters ensued. They came in force, presumptuous, hortatory. I had gone overseas in my country's name, a reassuring token of regularity. Annoying criticism shifted to annoying praise. Still nothing from E. The failure to face facts, I told myself, is the onset of dementia.

She had seen me off for San Francisco. Flustered by her first dramatic farewell, she had been unsure of every movement. She treated me as if I were a corpse and she a nervous child who didn't want to profane my funeral. As a friend was standing in the background, she was too shy with a kiss. "Goodby," she said softly, adding the diminutive of my name. It

17

was the first time I had heard it since childhood, and it was impossible to suppress a grimace.

Thinking back, I began to realize how thin our relationship had been. A friend had brought us together. His introduction had laid down parameters: I, rough-hewn, ruthless, with undeveloped tenderness; she, virginal, floral, with unexploited sensuality. My task, he had said with a poke to the ribs, was to control the fire I started. He told both of us the things that must be insinuated by months of blabber. Our acquaintance was able to be condensed. In a few weeks she and I issued a joint communiqué of intent.

But would she have waited until I left for lifting my illusions? It had seemed that we were drawing closer, within the limits of convention and morality. Had I been missing something? Tiny events may be fraught with great consequences. What recurring word might be stricken from our conversations? A modifier; a nuance of voice perhaps? Or had someone else appeared as I was swallowing powdered eggs? In an instant I saw that my judgment had been wrong in accepting her sentimental dialectic; I should have required her body.

Now it suggested the plight of the terminal case. The doctor assures him it is nothing serious. Family and friends concur; it is for the general good. Day by day, as his hold weakens, the patient must diagnose for himself. My universe stood corrected; E. was out of it. I began frequenting prostitutes. My life took on a seedy, diverted air. I hated E., and at once I knew that I had never loved her.

Her letters came at a blow. I lay prostrate on my bunk, taking gulps of air in the aftertaste of rice wine: it was Sunday morning. The mail clerk walked in and dumped them on the foot of my bed. I needed liquid to baste my throat, but feared the first swallow would

18

empty my stomach. For a moment I dreamed the mail clerk was an MP routing me from an illicit overnight. I sat up. So firm was my new scheme of things that I suspected her of changing her mind and forging a month of letters in an afternoon. I grabbed a letter. It was postmarked more than a month ago. Then I began to laugh, hurting my head with each concatenation.

The odyssey of the letters—a computer subroutine! They had been traveling an infinite loop. The iteration carried them to my original assignment, where the mail clerk stamped NO RECORD. Then back to the APO, where the words NO RECORD were lined out. And so again to the stated address. The program was literal in execution; the creators, too, were blameless: logic had not stumbled. In the end new orders had been put on file, debugging the routine. The number of iterations varied with the date of the letter. The one I picked up had crossed the ocean twenty-seven times.

E.'s love had circled; now arrived in port. I read the letters quickly, without chronology. Some noted my complaint about mail. I saw right away that nothing had been changed by their arrival. I did not love E.; I had never loved her.

I had no idea of what to do about her, and wished that, somehow, our pledges might themselves be trapped in a loop. I had not written lately, but the time lapse was within permissible limits. At least nothing offensive had been said. An infinite loop! It was then that I drafted a letter which I have been sending ever since with trivial modifications.

Dear E.,

Thank you for your beautiful letter. Your love sustains me in the lonely trial I am passing through. I often refer to your picture, and it brings to mind the gentle qualities that make you what you are. My feel-

ing for you has continued to mature with distance, and I await a chance to build the kind of life which two people seldom share.

Of my life here I can say little. One is not allowed to divulge all that he sees, and I would not do so if it were allowed. Do not, however, be concerned for my welfare. The hardships that you imagine are nothing.

I ask you only to continue waiting, loving, praying . . .

★ three ★

FULLY AWARE and unrepentant, I decided to carry on my shoulders a Pandora's bag, full of both virtues and vices from which I might add or delete selectively.

It was the habit of the married men to select a single prostitute and pay her by the month. This seemed a logical compromise halfway from chastity to license. The girls had come to accept the system and vied for the position of steady. Occasionally a single man made such a contract, fell in love, and eventually brought the girl stateside. A trip to the Big PX, as America was called, was the working girl's dream. To be like America-woman, they said, to smile with a tilted head and talk on the telephone. In hopes of this the steady girls did laundry for their men.

The girl I chose was from a group reported to decline offers from men not clean and tolerably attractive. They went for a premium. Her last steady had rotated, and she had been reduced to night-by-night teahouse work. We agreed to a date for testing out, with an option for permanent service. Once inside she ripped off her blouse to show me her large unbrassiered breasts. She described her trip to a doctor in Seoul who had injected them with foam. "Here, feel," she said, pulling my hands toward her chest and cupping them around the mounds. She smiled and lifted her chin, at the same time sucking in her stomach like a recruit. I cupped as she led, and expressed the expected appreciation. Not wanting to waste time looking, I made the bargain.

Each time we made love I intended to make a note in a log book. At the end of the month I would do a cost analysis to see if our arrangement was fair value. I bought a small notebook and recorded the date and number of times. The first weekend we observed a honeymoon.

A week later our unit took to the field on an alert. Our duty was to race to the top of a nearby mountain and set up an imaginary second line of defense. The advance unit would withdraw through us during the night, and we would withdraw through their lines the following day. My role in the retreat seemed self-explanatory, and I felt no need for practice. Someone at a higher echelon, however, felt the need to see it in flesh and steel. In their special way, the troops knew right away and went from barracks to barracks shouting, "It's a roundhouse. Joe hasn't jumped. Everybody cool." Joe being the yellow man on the target silhouettes.

The first night in the sleeping bag I felt the presence of a thousand crawling things. I slept in fits and starts and got up before dawn to urinate in the trench. It was a typical early morning trip, and I had fought it as long as I could. The cold made me hold my arms to my sides, yet I had to pry my shorts away from a moist warmth. A murky stream of yellow poured into the trench, and I reeled from hot pain. The rancid steam came sizzling up, confirming my diagnosis.

I told myself that gonorrhea is far from the worst. It is only a matter of going to the doctor and throwing yourself on his mercy. In a way, it is a relief to turn over responsibility for one's body. Not, of course, if the doctor is one of those who feels he must deliver a lecture on morality. He holds the specimen on a slide, his nose twitching in delighted disgust. For the moralists, sick people are a life-long vindication. The better ones make jokes. Venereal cases, after all, are their stock of professional humor. M.'s father, a successful surgeon, shakes his belly over "the drippers I dried up in the war." I can't begrudge him his laugh, especially as he tells in the next moment of the doctors marching out of step at their military graduation. And the lawyers shouting quack-quacks as they waited in line. Besides, doctors are not to be avoided. Saints or sinners, we are occasionally at their mercy.

The preventive medicine boys would be the rough ones. They would have me identify the girl from their cards and would round her up like a squad of gestapo. My telling would be "informing," and would terminate the contract. Fortunately she was to have been paid at the end of the month.

The other men would take it in the best spirits. It might even add to my standing, which could use some shoring up. If you're not a mixer it shows up right away in a quonset hut. With six bunks to the aisle, it's soon apparent that you prefer books. Such a person is tolerated so long as his aloofness applies equally to high and low.

My bunkmates were the sort who engaged in a lot of banter, manly braggadocio for the most part. The man in the next bunk liked to inform everyone of the profound impression his organ made on a steady girl. "Up the wall, up the wall when I hit her with it"— each night when he came in. It had never occurred to me to assert that I was a masculine man, or a brave man, for that matter. Both expressions struck me as tautological. Besides, someone was always laughing when I used the subjunctive. My silence was taken for reticence, and reticence for lack of enthusiasm. Now they would say, "Do you hear? 'Books' got himself a dose! 'Books' says he had a piece so good he's been coming for two weeks!"

Just so long as I did not have to tell them until I knew it was curable. Otherwise—if that should be the case. Then an alarming thought: I must inform the company commander! It was necessary to return to base for treatment. In a training lecture, with slides, it was stressed that our occupation had turned Korea into a laboratory. We had bred, with the help of camp-followers, a species of gonoccocus twenty times more resistant than the domestic strain. It demanded speedy treatment. Worse than that, since eighty percent of the GIs contracted it, it was such an embarrassment as to be monitored by command. A reported case is a black mark on the commander's record—charts and graphs are kept at headquarters. For the individual who contracted it, the next promotion could be denied.

I needed one more rank for duty in Vietnam. That is what the reply to my application had said. Outside of men sent in units, only rated personnel needed. Still, the matter of treatment was not to be escaped. Perhaps the doctor would treat it on the sly, once he understood my situation. At least I might avoid the stigma of asking to return in the middle of a field exercise.

I began with much resolve. It was like smashing a fist on the cabinet that bangs you. After two days I had to grip the handle of a watercan when passing water. A sudden spurt of urine, coming as I relieved my bowels, sent shock waves throughout my body. I stopped eating and drank only a cup a day. On the sly I went to the command tent and pressed the front of my body against the iron stove. A treatment used in the Middle Ages, it would at least forestall the culmination. At night, looking out on rows of mountains, like pew after pew of an open-air church, I had the cheap visions of the no-food-and-waterfalls mystic. In the morning nothing could be recalled of them.

As I told M., we live in peculiar times. Exterior walls have fallen. We must retreat to defend an inner citadel. It is a time for hiding deep beneath the skin, for choosing a self that is ultimately defensible. If only we were independent of our bodies! I recall the story of the Spartan boy, in whose upbringing theft—foraging, it is called—was inculcated as a way of life. The boy, having stolen a fox, was apprehended. Through his own clumsiness, no doubt. As he was questioned, he hid the fox beneath his coat. At the end of the interrogation, he fell dead at the magistrate's feet, the creature having devoured his guts.

First pain, then swelling testicles. Then a sensation of decay, of writhing maggots, in the lower stomach. At that point, conception is impossible. Instructions: don't get jostled, don't ride horses. I smiled. While the others rode in tanks or tracks, I trailed behind with low, plodding steps. Generals, I assumed, could not go on forever pinning flags on a board; I had seen old men at work. My shorts, including the extra set, grew foul with the putrefaction. Evidence of the conflict oozed out of me with increasing intensity. I felt like an aging corpse, the core beginning to decompose. A full week passed. I stood against a mountain pitted by barrages of the last war. A hostile nature had refused categorically to restore the trees. Not even seedlings interrupted the blasts of winter. I held the organ in my hand, ready for the daily ordeal. For no particular reason, I smiled. "Do you see, God? Do you note that I am rotting?" I smiled again, perhaps to show that one facial expression is as easy to come by as another.

We returned the next morning. The doctor refused clandestine treatment, but the leaders were grateful that I had waited until our return. I was only a month late in promotion. As soon as it came I filed another application. While I waited, I made the most of the dead time to schedule appointments with the dentist. Each day during the lunch hour I walked to headquarters to inquire if orders had arrived. A sergeant with a thin mustache turned me away from the door, outraged that I should trouble his routine with personal inquiries. But my persistence seemed to mellow him, and he allowed me to come inside only to repulse my questions with a daily joke. "Sorry," he said, "but the man you're going to replace hasn't been killed yet."

In recent days the sergeant had even taken to inviting me for a cup of the office coffee. Yesterday, he refused to speak to me, or even to admit to my presence in the room. After I had stood in front of his desk for some time, he reached down and handed me assignment orders. "Now get out!" he ordered. He went back to some very private and urgent work. For a moment I was caught completely off guard. I started to wheel around and speed away. Then I caught his point; he was thinking of the man we had caused to be displaced. "Don't blame me," I said turning back. "I didn't do it. If anyone . . ."

★ four ★

MY DEPARTURE was rather a staged event. A week before I was to leave, the unit bulletin noted: "It is hoped that all divisional personnel will take notice of the courage and devotion to duty of one of their comrades at arms." It went on to cite me by name and observe that I had volunteered for service in Vietnam not once but twice. This, it remarked, was evidence of a truly selfless and professional attitude. This observance sealed a final flush of good relations with my comrades. Until then a few of them had thought the idea of trying to get into combat somewhat asinine.

To my surprise the note was read virtually word for word at the conclusion of Saturday's battalion formation. Instead of reading my name, the battalion commander said "a certain man, whom I will not embarrass by naming, and who happens to be a member of this unit"; at this point, the platoon leader nodded in my direction and the other men turned around to look. Each officer in my chain of command—brigade, battalion, company, even the platoon leader—had been instructed to write a letter of commendation. Each said, as he tendered his, that the brigade commander thought it "the least we could do." The letter cited "the professionalism of service," a favorite theme in brigade publications. I filed the carbon copies as capital in future scrapes.

Each man came by to say goodby and assure me that, while they had not known me as well as they might have liked, they had always considered me a friend. Shaking hands with them, my mind was drawn to the fear all men have upon seeing one of their number sent to meet his fate. Promises of letters were exchanged, and addresses written on scraps of paper, to wrinkle in my wallet and be expunged the second or third time I had a housecleaning. Already I can hardly match names with faces. The following Monday I went back through the mountains to the replacement station where I had arrived. While there I sought out the sheets in my medical record concerning my recent illness: I burned them in a toilet stall and flushed the remainder down.

The next day I found myself in a group of seventy or eighty men milling around a giant jet. All were said to be volunteers. Here, I thought, would be persons like myself. I felt a rare receptivity for the sublime, the draconic, the mythically courageous. I studied faces, clothes, voices, bearing. It was inevitable that there be a common denominator, a kind of residue that had brought us to converge on this spot. In these men, perhaps, I might find a fuller rendition of my own character. So completely lost did I become in my examination that I wandered out of the crowd and very nearly missed the command to board. From a distance, neither the faces nor figures were robust in a youthful way. Some had sunken-chested tubercular frames, a look of being used. Others, while better padded out, did not match my conception of the sinewy warrior. For one thing, they were older than I had expected, a few in the late twenties, but most in the thirties and forties.

As an amateur among professionals, I was twice

aroused. Seen from a distance, the mélange of ribbons and decorations graved a testimonial in abstract. I imagined that the faces hid experience and tragedy. Behind their reticence would be the hard-earned wisdom of the man of action, hidden with the tenacity by which the professional keeps his secrets. Technical men hate amateurs. A sneer is never entirely absent from their faces when they address outsiders. Men who fix cars must at bottom realize that for their function to exist, other men must break cars and become frustrated. Yet down deep one suspects that they never feel quite the same about a person when they learn that his life is not devoted to engines.

As we moved to board, I took a closer look. It was in my mind to reconstruct careers, station to station, by the overseas ribbons and service medals. The truth hit me at once! Not one of the ribbons was for combat; they were peacetime soldiers! Entering service at the end of the Korean war, they were the oldest men in the service not to have had a war. Far from being the hard cases who had begun to awe me, they were merely intruders, taking a last charge in a war that belonged to my generation. Perhaps it was a gamble for promotion before my age group overtook them. They had a look about them, old and resigned, as if headed for the last place on earth where they might yet make another rank.

Abruptly my attitude changed. With the new insight I began to see double chins, drunkards' noses, bellies overhanging trousers. They had grown soft in confidence that they were machines to perform their function. They had cast their lots with the super bombs and had expunged traditional virtues from the books. My reason punished them with the spite reserved for errant mechanics. Then, again, my feelings mellowed. They had entered, they believed, a uniformed branch of the civil service, but suddenly were being made to fight for their careers. As if to ratify my judgment, a hand touched my shoulder, the tentative intention of camaraderie by which an aging spectator hails an athlete. Turning to join the line, I found a portly colonel looking me in the eye. He gave my shoulder a fatherly shake and lamented that it was a small war, but the only one we've got.

The flight to Vietnam was a too-perfect resumption. As the first tray of eggs arrived, I felt like giving my arm a pinch. Perhaps I could ask the man in the next seat if he had just spent a tour in Korea. I awaited the first twinges of the toothache, then placed my finger on the molar and saw that it was filled.

In my student days I had been compelled to take extended trips by bus. It soon became difficult to tell if the bus was an interlude in my life, or my life an interruption of the bus. Suddenly it became tempting, as the bus pulled up for a three A.M. rest stop, to say, "Excepting my imagination—a ninety-minute stop, a talk with a stranger, a littered floor, a new driver, and a resumption: these are everything." Reaching my destination, I was welcomed in familiar arms and put away to bed, only to resume traveling in flatland between Cleveland and Chicago. And just when the last trip was forgotten another began. Much of life, it seemed, was a search for the way to pinch oneself and be sure that the pinch itself is not contained in a dream.

Yesterday, for a moment, it seemed that the pinch had arrived. As the stewardess was removing the last tray of eggs, the pilot notified us that he was shutting off all lights. Because of sniper fire, we would approach the airport in blackout and be met by a helicopter gunship. Out of my window I could see tiny sparks on the ground. We were not to be alarmed at

30

the steep descent, which was another precaution due to the extraordinary circumstances.

"Extraordinary circumstances" seemed to be just the needed phrase. I felt vastly reassured. I reasoned that when events are unexpectedly complex—that is, when they appear beyond the power of the unaided imagination—you can be relatively certain of their reality. It's as if they were too difficult for a prankster to invent. I felt exhilarated at the airport, and later as a bus carried us through predawn Saigon. I could already make out an architecture full of grillwork balconies and walled gardens. Such an arrival seemed unquestionable. I slept without dreams.

★ five ★

On waking I felt less certain. For one thing, it was evening, and the repetitiveness of dark had begun to bore in on my nerves. For another, I felt no different than I had in Korea. It was, true, unusually warm, particularly for the evening. But for a traveler changes in weather become a matter of course. I tried sleeping again, but when I finally dropped off, I found myself back aboard the aircraft. Then I was hurried down to breakfast.

Our group is staying at the Kolper, which is reserved to men in advisory elements. It is a small white hotel down the street from the purple pastel Hoa Lu. The colors remind me of the pastel reservations for old folks in Florida. The layout, however, is like New Orleans, the quarter where Vieux Carré the Explorer, fortified with French art and Napoleonic drive, stumbled on a new world. There and here are stucco buildings, ironwork walls, enclosed gardens, and of course the ceiling fans. There and here are wooden shutters and long open balconies. I call it French colonial, a logical enough name for the laymen, but probably not what the architects call it.

It was apparent from the gathering at breakfast that I was to be processed along with the others from the plane. Those in charge of processing, except for the tropical cut to their uniforms, were the same as the ones who processed us out in Korea. At the station in Korea, the initial briefing had contained the warning, "Gentlemen, I need not caution you that getting frostbite is against regulations. It is considered destruction of government property." This morning the sergeant in charge began, "Gentlemen, I need not caution you that getting sunburn is against regulations. It is considered destruction of government property."

As in Korea, we have been warned against the local women. Statistics were cited. In any event, we have been told, if determined to establish liaison, use a condom. The officer giving the lecture, as in Korea, was a tall, pale major. He had sunken cheeks. He warned against using the prophylactics manufactured on the local market. They are frequently retreads, and in any case are not designed for giants from the West. The American model, he assured, is available in every orderly room; such logistical precaution is required for races so richly endowed. I thought of this man as Major Gulliver. I wondered if he himself had a full issue of personal equipage. He gave us cards with ten rules of conduct to follow in the country. We are not to argue in public, or to insult women.

The others have noticed the buildings. They are pleasantly surprised with at least one aspect. They proclaim the setting exotic; inwardly they exult in its familiarity. There is hope, they think, because it looks like Florida. It is the stucco and the pastels. My sympathy with them has waned. They will curse this land for a year because today it turned their faces green. They do not differentiate between the malice of foreign microbes and their need for the anesthetically familiar.

They do not notice when the sun bounces up in the morning and collapses in a heap at night: a tropical phenomenon, you can look it up in a book. There is

33

no miracle in a tropical orange sun. Nor in the equatorial effect of evenly divided night and day. We of the temperate zones are accustomed to lingering clichés of dawn and dusk. We catch newspaper notices of longest and shortest days. Often even these slip by. When we travel south to days of mathematical regularity, born and consumed in orange fire, or north to the white sun and unceasing day or night above the ice, we say, "My God, the mosquitos!"; "My God, the wasteland!"

We are near enough to the equator here that seasons are wet and dry. Dry, it was said in the briefing, are preferable for helicopter operation; wet brings out the flying bugs. All is attributable to wind currents. As to the punctuality of dawn and nightfall, I mentioned it to a group of the men outside the classroom. They shrugged as if embarrassed. A captain who happened to have studied geography made his hands into a globe and explained the inevitability of it.

I understood then what it means to belong to a race which confines itself to answers. Never have there been men with less curiosity. If the world be proven paradoxical, I thought, the next morning will find them huddled beneath the sheets.

M. expects, and, I think, hopes, that I am going to unravel. He thinks it inevitable, as he is sure that I have psychological reasons for being here. After all, he pointed out, how else can a member of a pacifist society find himself in the next breath serving in a war?

That, I told him, is precisely the point. I am here to demonstrate the possibility of my being here. Besides, the war is an interim event. When I return, I can seek forgiveness prodded by the maturity and sensitivity I stand to gain. This explanation was not acceptable to M. No one in his right mind does things to bear out a philosophic principle. Further, I am too intelligent to share the mundane motives of my compatriots. All the more necessity, I said.

M. takes great liberties by way of the rights as my best friend. He expects to be informed not only of what I do, but of the components which make it possible. He wants to know me so that each of my actions becomes inevitable. He believes that men do not really make decisions. If I am converted, for instance, he is unimpressed. The act of converting makes one less a disciple than a changer of sides.

In a sense M. is undoubtedly right. I make decisions, but I never feel that they are decisions. They always seem either self-evident or the product of a coin flip, decided by the density of air. Either the numbers decide for me, or a shrug sees me by. It's almost as if I were watching another person who also happens to be myself. M. claims that being in the service is a self-inflicted psychological joke.

I told him before leaving that I have watched myself at work for close onto twenty-one years, and have a fair idea of how I will respond to any given situation. Sometimes I act differently just to break the monotony. This, too, is becoming a pattern. At least I got out of the country and it hasn't cost me a jail term.

Then, of all things, he wanted me to write articles of exposé for an underground paper. He was planning to put a paper out for army personnel. I was having none of that. When I'm through, I said, the army will owe me all sorts of things, some of which I can't even name as yet. M. was disappointed, but to be honest one of the things I had most felt like escaping was roommates who keep sending you down to the hardware store for curtain rods or some such, because it's your turn. Myself I don't need curtains. If I feel the need, I imagine them, and from that time on they are there.

35

All day today, the men from the plane have been speculating about assignments. The colonel who put his hand on my shoulder was among the first to find out. He lit up completely upon learning that his tour would be spent in Saigon. And on the Joint Staff! No danger, and perhaps a chance to assemble credentials for his first star. They say that once you get the first star, the rest comes easily. As the day wore on, his figure stiffened and he grew more guarded among the men. He crept away at lunch to change into a freshly starched uniform.

Of my own assignment, I have learned nothing. This much I did learn: the dental service is well represented in every corps. This project may continue.

★ six ★

LOOKING AT the wall map, I read off the names: Duc Hoa, Tuy Hoa, My Tho, Dong Tam, Cai Be, Nam Can, Cai Cai, Bac Lieu . . . Can Tho. I asked myself what I had expected. The building of a wooden horse? Its infiltration? A consummation in which I sprang from its belly at night to massacre sentinels and spoil provisions? My orders said that I was to be a clerk. As headquarters clerk in Fourth Corps, I would oversee paperwork having to do with the towns I had read off. The headquarters itself was in Can Tho. Attached to the orders was a note from someone at central assignment. "How about this, comrade. Welcome aboard. Glad to be of service to you, and best of luck!" It was unsigned.

The briefing sergeant knew little of that headquarters. Perhaps it was sufficiently beleaguered as to constitute a de facto combat assignment. He thought not. "The native commander is supposed to have worked out some sort of truce with the enemy. Under the table, of course. The worst you'll get down there is butt-end boils."

The thought came to me of simply deserting and walking beyond the edge of town until I found the action. Of course this made no sense. The whole idea of this interlude was to apply my aggression in a constructive cause, a cause with social sanction. I recalled the ordeals of training. At various times, I had rappelled from cliffs, learned Morse code, and qualified in jumping from planes. The worst of it had been the jumping, not the fear itself, but the uncertainty created by having men of unknown quality to each side. It could be sticky if the man ahead flinched in the door. Luckily I had managed to disturb the incompetent fellow in front of me until he quit the training. Then there had been the classes in making explosive charges with soap dishes.

There had, of course, been the note. Someone had written it, even though he remained nameless. There had been a personal hand in my assignment. It was just possible, if this was true, that the same hand could effect a change. After all, the tone of the note had suggested an intent to be obliging.

The central assignment building looked from the outside like a warehouse. Its geometric regularity suggested enormous quantities of raw space. The first glimpse inside produced a striking effect. There were no partitions dividing it, or rather, only one insignificant one at the far end, setting apart the senior officers. Desks, deserted and occupied, were lined up by the dozens of rows. Images flashed by; block upon block of shotgun houses in a low-income subdivision, pews in a huge church, a scene of mass petting and near copulation at a party.

When I asked a stray clerk where to find the section for Fourth Corps, he suggested that I walk a few rows in a certain direction and ask again. This happened twice more, sending me in a zigzag pattern, before I reached a neighborhood where specific instructions were possible. I saw a sign suspended from the ceiling, IV CORPS ADV TM. Underneath it were four desks with the corps emblem. They were arranged in diamond configuration within the long rows. One was occupied by a junior enlisted man.

Displaying my orders with the note pointed toward him, I asked if he might know the author. "I might and I might not," he replied. When I told him I needed to speak to the author, he was quick to inform me that adjustments were against policy. The word "change" was not even spoken inside the building. I invited him out for a drink.

Drink in hand, he readily admitted to being the author of the note. Before I could get around to the subject of my assignment, he asked, "Do you believe in evolution?"

I told him that I did; I had studied it in college. His eyes brightened, and his voice shifted into a secretive tone. He leaned forward as if addressing a member of a cabal. His pointing finger made an arc of the bar.

"Savages," he said. "Prescientific! Do you get me? They don't know the most elemental things. Darwin. Huxley. You and I are different."

I leaned forward to emphasize that we had a shared point of view. He continued with his theory.

It's impossible, he told me, to practice evolution on any sort of scale. His finger again swept the bar. One does the best he can. Certain situations provide more opportunity than others for putting one's ideas into practice. Take for instance the Fourth Corps personnel function. Did I get his point? Eugenics might be practiced there, if only in a small way. Still, he was making the earth a better place, and how many men could say that?

He had devised a system whereby the men with GT scores below 110 were given the combat jobs. Higher scores brought progressively safer duty. He had to remind me that the GT was a sort of combined index for ability with words and numbers. Being assigned to headquarters, he assured me, implied that I was among the most intelligent men in the corps. Of all the corps, he repeated. A number of the junior fellows there are really quite bright. If figures were collected in this regard, a good many senior officers would be embarrassed. He knew.

While nodding affirmation, I took advantage of a pause to explain my personal need with regard to assignment. I stressed the point that my position was exceptional. His expression changed abruptly, and he sat back in his chair, erasing the confidential posture.

"I realize, Specialist, that your motives in requesting a change of assignment are uncommon. All the same, it is not possible to make an exception. Nature does not make exceptions. Think of the precedent. In fact, artificial exceptions is one of the shortcomings of the human species.

"The beauty of the system is that it has no special cases. Do you realize that all I must do is depart once, just once, and I will never again be able to say that I make no exceptions?"

My face must have assumed a surly look, for he continued in a gruffer voice. Never mind, he said, that he and I were of the same rank. It was a matter of position. It was hardly his fault that there weren't enough combat jobs to go around. I should note that in any situation of scarcity a political necessity arose for someone to sit at the head of the table and dispose. Our ranks notwithstanding, he sat in that chair. It was my duty to abide by his judgment, and duty failing, I would abide anyway because I had no choice.

The following day I began again at central administration. This time I found a senior enlisted man. So I was to be a clerk, he observed. I should be proud. He had spent twenty years as an army clerk, and took pride in every moment. He could understand my vexation if I had set my heart on something else, but

I would grow accustomed to it. The role was not without rewards, whatever one's personal interests. He cited the case of a Southern fellow in Germany who had resegregated an entire armored division. The pattern was discovered at inspection; the Third Brigade stood up and it looked like an apple tree with blackbirds roosting. He tried to impart at once the humor, the mistakenness of principle, and the technical achievement. Further downgrading of the clerical function on my part, he made clear, would be taken as an affront to his chosen profession.

On the other hand, he was totally sympathetic with my grievance. The matter would be looked into. Of course, *my* orders could not be changed. This was against policy. However, if the clerk involved were found to be controverting official guidelines, I could rest assured that he would be dealt with. This was a separate question entirely from my assignment, which was already settled, and I should desist from efforts to muddle the issues. His face grew intensely reflective, as if he were straining to encompass both sides of an argument.

Not a bad idea, though, he said. You might say that these mothers with the high IQs were a national resource. Yes, that was undoubtedly the way his subordinate was looking at it. Of course, that might not be policy, and the matter bore looking into. Nevertheless, it certainly made no sense to have your scarce resources getting their ass shot off in paddies.

★ seven ★

THE BUILDINGS are stucco, the architecture French. Like the rest of the country, Can Tho is capable of both hybrid grace and provincial lack of taste. The compound where I work is a miniature stucco fortress, put up more for the illusion of security than the reality. The reality is provided by elite troops who are stationed in a ring around the capital. Also, some say, by a bargain involving as quid pro quo the chief enemy stronghold.

I live in one compound, work in another. Both are enclosed and patrolled by guards. The compound where I sleep is a fenced rectangle, built as a French villa, but now housing four hundred personnel. It has been enlarged by adding rows of tropical rooms with the upper walls of fine screen. My room is the next-to-last compartment of the third row on the enlisted side. My roommate, T., has been here for eight months. A member of the radio section, he happens to work nights; I seldom see him. Our presence coincides only in the early morning when he comes in, or at lunch, if I happen to return to the compound. The bed is a double-decker, and since T. is on the heavy side, he shakes it with two or three ponderous blows when he comes in. From the start he has been friendly, eager to show me the ropes. He greeted me, and still greets me, by saying. "This is a bitch here, boy, but we make the most of it." His habitual comment in warm weather has to do with how good a beer will taste. When I come in at lunch, he is likely to look up from his bed, where by right of tenure he has the lower bunk, and announce that it is good sleeping weather. He is referring to the gentle tapping of rain on the roof.

I am becoming acclimated to his possessions, which decorate the room. For me, that is, they are décor. To him, they are property. Pasted on the back of the door is a large sticker in our national colors with the words FUCK COMMUNISM. The signs were made by a leftist group back home which intended to perpetrate a satire. The effort failed, and T. displays his deadpan as a statement on politics. Each day as I close the door, I notice the bright contrast of the colors. The paints must have been treated with the same material as iridescent clock hands.

On the wall opposite the beds is a calendar girl. There is no calendar underneath her. She is printed on rice paper, and her body, rather than being glossy, is pulpy and filled with squares. She is drawn to comic-strip proportions. There are three hundred sixty-five of the squares. About half of them are colored with red pencil. I have discovered that T. colors one a day. She is "his short-timer calendar," he says. Upon close examination, I found that the numbers progress along paths and detours to the dark triangle where the thighs meet. As I get into bed, I cannot fail to notice her. I think of prisoner-of-war movies. The hero under torture builds a house in his imagination brick by brick. In it he places his wife, his children, their toys and pets. I think also of the Japanese colonel, scowling, aware that his bearded, starving prisoner has access to invincible, unseen moral support.

The room at night is strewn with magazines. Although they are girlie magazines, I never find them open to pages containing nudes. Usually they are pressed face down on the bed, open to a story illustrated by a combat scene. I read one of the stories, which proved to be a factual account of the deaths of several Nazi generals and the escape of another with his mistress.

Although T. has a Spanish name, he has informed me that he is not Puerto Rican. His ancestry is Mexican and Indian. He plans to marry a girl from his town, although he hasn't decided which of two, and then he will raise cattle. When I told him of my desire to see combat, he informed me flatly that I was crazy. To mitigate the impression I had made, assuming that I would be living with him for some time, I told him that I came from a family with a long military tradition. Valor is expected of me. He could understand that very well and wished me luck.

The buildings where I work have an aura of intrigue—high ceilings, slow-turning fans, and the ever-present material which seems applied by dirt daubers. One must imagine a corrupt gendarmerie and a contingent of veteran poules with profound underlying humanity. These would complete the romantic setting. Instead, the buildings are occupied by men with papers in their hands. Someone is always walking rapidly, extending his natural step, to take a handful of paper from one building to another.

My immediate superior is a Negro master sergeant. In three years of consecutive overseas service he has outlasted an unwanted wife and impregnated three local girls. Each of whom now draws a fair fraction of his paycheck. He does not believe this arrangement, forced by superiors, will stand up once he is back in the states. He has not contested it as long as he is here. His contribution to the war has been a comprehensive filing system for G-3. It is efficient and effortless, with a touch of the sublime. He can lay his finger instantly on any wanted document. No one else can find anything. A month or so ago an old man ran afoul of Sergeant R., who was executing a typically daredevil maneuver in the office jeep. He had his current girl along. This incident is the cause of his precipitate departure, which will take place next week. The old man died. R.'s only comment to me has been, "Make yourself at home. This is your office now. Enjoy it while you are here." The plans officer, referring perhaps to the file system, said in a breach of usual military courtesy, "I don't know how we'll ever get along without Sergeant R., but we'll sure be delighted to try."

The plans officer himself is leaving in a few weeks, to his great satisfaction. Major DeL. is an example of a phenomenon occurring only in our country by which a miner's son, himself marked to be a miner, cannot only hold a commission but walk around with a name misplaced generations ago by a member of the exiled nobility. Sunken-chested and -cheeked, weak-eyed, poorly educated, proletarian in a word, DeL. is the subject of one more irony; he appears to be an excellent officer. He has planned as well as possible, and, if asked, would have died the same way. Since he won his commission from the ranks, he can be no more than a lieutenant colonel. He seems to be the man who holds the section together.

The man whose duty it is to hold it together is Colonel Y., formerly Lieutanant Colonel Y., who received a promotion during my first week. Y. makes no distinction between personal and unit triumphs, so in spite of the fact that I had been in the office only three days, I was allowed to participate in his promotion every bit as much as the rest of the staff. Everyone assumed a modest fixed smile. Too great a smile, everyone seemed to sense, would be construed as satirical. A straight face would imply envy, dislike, or indifference. I watched their faces wriggle into position and imitated them. Each in order of decending rank filed by to congraulate the colonel. I filed by. I was dispatched to purchase the new insignia. I saw that each word of praise be garnered, including the festivity at his departure, would be shared with each of us.

Each departure is festive in its own way. Since there has been no mass homecoming, it seems that each individual's leaving must represent a victory in miniature. Since the rotations after one-year tours are staggered, victory is a continuous process. It is thus more sustained than the sword tendering, paper signing, and ticker-tape marching of previous wars. On the other hand, it is followed by an equally continuous reappraisal. Newcomers are always groaning that "that bastard left me in a bind."

The section is being rocked by three successive departures, my predecessor, Sergeant R., and Major DeL. And before too long Colonel Y. as well. The implication of this is clear. At the beginning of the week I requested permission to speak with Colonel Y. concerning transfer. Sergeant R. and Major DeL. agreed that transfer was prefectly all right as far as they were concerned. Colonel Y., while agreeing to take the matter under advisement, brought up the point that I am asking transfer from a unit already decimated. He is unwilling to make a commitment. In fact, within fourteen days, he points out, I alone will know the combination of the safe.

Yesterday a most distressing encounter added insult to injury. A functionary of the Red Cross appeared at my door to ask that I write my parents. When I attempted to be noncommittal, he demanded it. Until that moment, it had not crossed my mind that I hadn't written. The debacle in Korea had soured me on mail.

46

At the same time, I realized that it was fitting; I had nothing to say. The Red Cross, who has officer standing, was dissatisfied with this response. My parents had written faithfully. I admitted it. I remembered their letters.

The letters berated me as the first in a long line to serve as less than an officer. Also for being the first to participate in an apparently losing war. What were we up to over here, they wanted to know? If we couldn't squelch a ragtag peasant revolt, what were young people coming to? The old man had sprung to his country's defense as a man of breeding should, that is, as an officer aboard a transport. He had followed the flag to victory. He could not understand following the flat to stalemate. As they story went, told in impeccably manful idiom, the fellow next to him "had got a chunk of his butt shot off at Leyte and received a Purple Heart for his trouble. But for the grace of the Almighty . . ." In spite of the near miss, the old man had endured, returned, conceived, and gone forth again. His son was born while he was at sea. Being the night decoding officer, he slept from noon until midnight. He napped from eight A.M. until noon. He was waked only for news of the atomic bomb on Hiroshima; he wished it luck, turned over, and returned to the land of dreams. Such were the men I chose to slight. I stood in underwear at my door and was threatened by the Red Cross.

My parents had contacted the Secretary of the Army. They had used an elected official as intermediary. They insisted that I was dead, and that no one had had the courtesy to report it. They would not be reassured otherwise until they had in their hands a personal letter. My father, said the Red Cross, was some sort of big shot, and big shots could command letters from their sons whenever they wished. It would go hard for me until I cranked one out.

47

It seemed too bad that, in drawing up the letter for E., I had not arrived at a form which would cover relatives and friends as well. It occurred that I could yet do so. I could bribe the mimeograph clerk to make the copies. But I thought better of it. It is possible that in my current frame of mind I would commit indiscretions. Who knows but that the recipients might be the very people I would need someday when I ran for Congress? The advantages in life, I have learned, are with people as mute as cabbages.

The Red Cross persevered. One expects hardships at war, I said, but he expects compensations. Was Nicias required to write his mother while leading the Athenians to slaughter? Far from it, the reward for dying in Sicily was escape from decaying Athens.

Was I being impudent, the Red Cross inquired, and if so did I realize that he had the power to order me sent to a border outpost? There I would be glad enough to exchange mail with my family and pray once a month when the chaplain was helicoptered in. This idea gave me a flicker, but I knew that Colonel Y. would never allow it. Instead there would be questionings and lectures. In the end I would be compelled to write. I made it easy for myself.

Dear Parents,

How are you? I am fine. The war, too, is fine. You will pardon me for not writing. I have been the victim of a recurrent . . .

★ eight ★

THE MATTER OF TEETH is pressing forward. This morning was my first appointment since arriving in country. Another slash mark on my chart, and a cleaning to boot. I rather enjoy the grinding away. It takes my mind off things. Futhermore, it is good evidence to being awake. In a way, my life seems to proceed from dental chair to dental chair.

As I waited in the outer office, I watched the dentist's technician, a native girl of twenty-five or so. She was minding both the reception desk and her infant son. The boy was dressed in a kind of shirt, or skirt, which left him nude from the waist down. She was caressing him with sensual strokes. At the end of a gliding touch, she grasped his small penis gently between two fingers and ended by rolling back the foreskin. The tot was squealing with joy. I wondered if I were watching planted the seeds of homosexuality or the vital lust of a satyr. Whatever future it augured, the caress seemed natural and quite what the child wished. The gentle, sliding motion drew my attention to the absence of a wedding ring. I found myself fighting an erection.

I sat down in a chair surrounded by gadgets and waited for the doctor to appear. To my surprise, he stepped in only to wash his hands and then left. The girl came instead, and with her eyes focused on the roof of my mouth, began to buff my teeth with intense concentration. She complimented me on their excellent condition, and I felt a moment of self-congratulation for my morning brushings. With vanity I thought of the white impression they made against my tanned face. As she worked, she let her breasts rotate against my chest and shoulders. Cleaning teeth is not an easy occupation for one who is less than five feet tall. Yet I am convinced the gesture was intentional and even fancy that I could feel the nipples grow taut through her silk blouse. Still, it was not at all a come-on. It was more a sort of spur-of-the-moment gift, the reward for a clean and beautifully attended mouth.

Last weekend the word got around that a comedian of great standing was coming to entertain in the corps. This struck me as odd. The man in question is known as the Christmas comedian, and it is nowhere near Christmas. He appears with a troupe of girls and a selection of bawdy material. His staple is to call an ungainly soldier to the stage and have him stand where he must look down a starlet's dress. While this is going on, the comedian addresses the audience with small obscenities.

On Monday morning I learned that the rumor of a visitor was true. All personnel were expected to attend the show. I went to Colonel Y. and asked special permission to absent myself.

"Am I understanding," said the colonel, "that this fellow has come ten thousand miles, and risked his ass, to tell you a joke, and you would rather sit on your butt and read a book?"

That was the size of it, I said. The colonel said he suspected me of intending to return to my room and sack out. This, I admitted, might well be a part of

50

my agenda. Although he considered my argument diluted by this admission, he did not want to seem arbitrary in his answer. Let us reason it out, he said.

"Look at it this way. Where would we be if everybody wanted to go to their rooms when famous comedians had come all that way? What if nobody showed up to hear the poor son-a-bitch? How would he feel? How would *we* look?

I had to admit that would make for a poignant turn of events. He seemed to think that the matter was settled until I said, "Well? Do I, or do I not, have to go?" This put him in a dudgeon. I was being illogical, and he liked to work things out by reason. He would have to think it over now. On the one hand, he would hate to see the argument go beyond the two of us. On the other, a concession could easily set off a chain reaction.

Later in the afternoon he announced that he had had time to consider the ramifications. If I wished to be rude, there was nothing to be done about it. Our society hoped to teach the precept of courtesy, but one of the aspects of a free society was that it did not force certain rules upon recalcitrants. One of the things that we did not do was force our soldiers to attend performances by comedians. I congratulated myself, saluted, and turned to leave. ". . . on the other hand," he caught me at the door, "the general has brought up the point that we need an enlisted escort for the party of a guest." My services had been volunteered. I was well-spoken and big enough to carry suitcases and stage equipment. The fact that I did not care for the comedian was an added boon in that it assured that I would not be bothering him with questions.

*

For three days I carried his bags and loaded them on airplanes to locations in the Delta. To my surprise, my surly expression did not meet with disapproval.

51

The comedian thought me a combat hero who had won under fire the privilege of being his valet. I stood a few step to the rear of the general and the comedian. They spoke as if I were not present. The precedent for this was established. The comedian had shaken my hand with a very final hello. I like to meet the troops, wherever they are from, he told the general. Yes, the general agreed, they are all alike. The comedian asked if I were a combat hero. The general said yes, that I had put my life on the line dragging a wounded buddy to safety. The comedian nodded gravely. They engaged in small talk.

The general was deferential to the comedian, which surprised me until I remembered one of M.'s pronouncements. M. claims that all military men, no matter how successful, are certain in their hearts that they could not make it anywhere else. This is supposed to account for their awe before successful politicians and businessmen. They never fully accept the fact that the awe goes the other way too. Before retiring, they speak bravely of redirecting talents, but when offered jobs as executives or political offices, they believe it pure largess.

The comedian was assuring the general that he had never regretted touring bases. Somehow he had grown in wealth and standing in spite of the lost time. On one occasion, his absence on a junket had prevented his making a grave mistake in the stock market. God and country watch over those who . . . It had been his pleasure to huck a few bonds in time of national trial. In times without trial as well. That was when many, otherwise patriotic, let down. He never forgot the men in uniform. And yet, it seemed that the years he had put in on the road, so to speak, had taught him where to put his money. It went to show . . .

The general nodded; money, says M., appears to the soldier a sort of contemporary manna. Since he has nothing to do with the system of real production, he must assign to real goods a metaphysical origin.

Taking a look back at me, the comedian stated that he had no special affinity for heroes. To his mind, all the men were equal. The general nodded.

"You're absolutely right about that," he said. "The individual hero, we have a way of saying, is obsolete. I've always said myself that all men are equally commendable. Except for a few rotten apples, of course. You might even say that the more common the job, the more the man is a hero. At least that's our way of thinking here. To the best of our ability we show no partiality."

The comedian went on with homilies about the free enterprise system, and people who wanted their share without pulling their load. "I say, if a man wants something, he's got to have something to swap for it. You take me . . ." I noticed that the general had a habit of nodding before the comedian reached the predicate of his sentence. Every now and then, the comedian would say, "The fact is . . ." and the pause would catch the general with his head bobbing up and down, "Yes, yes."

This coming Monday the new operations sergeant is to arrive. Colonel Y. has told me that his name is Mooney and that I am to show him the ropes. He is to be my immediate superior, and it is obvious to Y. that no one else is as well equipped to inform him of his task. This weekend I am to work day and night to catch up.

★ nine ★

MOONEY ARRIVED as scheduled and for several days had a newcomer's deference. On his face is a fixed expression of the small man's burden. It contains the lost promotion and the small-town divorce with seedy revelations. It never changes. When he smiles or speaks, there it is: the bellyache wince. In a way his expression follows the expression of all regular army men. All are capable of one basic emotion. They maintain it on their faces at all times. It may be a grin through which they scowl, or a wince through which they must transact smiles. I have added a new measure of humanity: diversity of emotion which can be expressed in the face.

Mooney nevertheless is an interesting sample. His first response to the office was that it seemed to have a pretty smooth operation. All it lacks, he said, is a little leadership. He remained in this cocoon for two weeks, until he felt he grasped the essentials, or until I had twice declined his offers of a drink. I am not sure which.

The he called me aside for a man-to-man chat. He began by stating that while I am not a regular, he felt the potential most definitely there. If I consigned myself to his hands, he was sure that I could be regularized within the period of a tour. What is more,

I could be promoted. It was a matter of recognizing the comradely relations which are maintained among fellow noncoms. It was also a matter of renouncing the civilian way of thinking. He did not know how best to put it. I recalled a cadre sergeant in training who kept asking me if I were out of my *military* mind. Mooney was prepared to be a father to me, he said, if I would let him. I thanked him without emotion and offered my hand. It was rendered as a member of the nobility expecting a commoner's kiss. A frown was superimposed on Mooney's wince. That afternoon, as I left the office, he called out, "Boysan, you will wear your headgear at all times when out of doors. As per army regulations."

My convalescent hours are spent at a library. For some reason there is a library on the sleeping compound allocated to the Naval Advisory Team. This team consists of two officers and three sailors who advise the riverboat force. The library is open to all the men on the compound by order of the general, who holds temporary power over the sailors. In going there night after night I have met a girl.

Lwan appeared gradually. I cannot draw a line saying, "There I was aware of her; before that, not." Maybe there were no first words at all, but indifference, which then was a nod of the head, which then was a nightly routine. Certain beginnings are like the border sorties of an expanding empire seen a hundred years retrospective. Questions of origin are no longer paramount; that is a Westerner's way of saying it. Things happen and are forgotten. My uncle swears that in each war a man must be found to fire the first shot. The Asians, on the other hand, refuse to divide life into fragments; to them the fragments do not actually exist, no more than time on a clock. They glide into rooms without the appearance of taking steps and their histories do not record the names of obscure sergeants who lit off first volleys.

The library houses five thousand books, give or take a few. Three quarters of them are mysteries or Westerns. Most of the others are how-to books with a median age of about twenty years. How to make a killing on stocks and bonds in 1925, for instance. The remainder are books of tactics and strategy. These are checked out by officers in a pattern suggesting that they are required reading, at least in a quasi-official way. When they are returned, the words in italics are also underlined.

The library contains three novels by Hemingway, under single cover, a Faulkner, a few biographies, a reference section, and Gide's *Corydon*. The Gide has captured my imagination because of its unlikely setting. It has been checked out a number of times, but returned the next day. There is evidence that borrowers erase their names. A defense of deviates is, of course, an anomaly here. I often wonder what forces came into confluence for its presence. Do anomalies impair or reinforce authenticity? It is a small question to the professional philosophe, but one with special meaning for me. Each room I enter seems perfectly natural until I observe that I am in it. At that point it becomes singular, the more singular when I observe that I am pondering its singularity. And consequently taking artificially contrived actions.

The girl presents a problem. As soon as I noticed her, I wanted her. Left to dwell on this a night or two, I wanted her with considerable determination. Then the game began. I kept wanting to say, "Look here. Let's off to a private place and get with it!" It is not to be done that way.

As a matter of fact, I have a very good idea of the percentages. Somewhere I heard the story of the man who got slapped accosting on the street corner. He told the bystander, "But I get a lot of the other stuff too!" I tried it at a party; the percentage is exactly zero. As I thought of it, this result made good sense. Our species has added a web of metaphysical associations to the sex act. What could I expect? The girls knew nothing of my motives, my composition. Probing for a data base, I revised my approach slightly at each successive party. The upshot was that I soon returned to the same insinuations, the same lies, promises, and false patience, as I had used before; as everyone uses. Perhaps it is a vindication of folk wisdom.

M. would be upon me again. If he read thoughts. Retrograde, rightist tendencies on the subject of sex. Revisionism. An admission of contradictions among the people. I should tell him that I too would like an ideal world. I would prefer to spend my life being accepted freely when sexual schedules permitted. But this is not Utopia! If they are going to be stubborn and hypocritical, so am I.

This case is going to be harder than most. To dissimulate successfully, one must first know what he is, or rather what he appears; then what the customer wants. Being an anomaly creates problems. It's like being unidentifiable by your own agents. She must be shown not the reality, not an adjustment of the reality, but an adjustment of her illusion. An American, a soldier, an enlisted man; the scum of the foreigners' garbage. The burden of proof is on me.

In her country soldiers are an elite. Rank is fluid, depending upon plots, bribes, and exploits. There is no excuse for a person like me. The concept of a civil service army is alien. Such words as tenure, seniority, bureaucracy have no meaning. I cannot simply explain away what I am. To tell her who I am is impossible. Our system, for decades triumphant, is still unappreciated in theory. Family wealth alone should have made me a general. Bravery a major general. Conspiracy a lieutenant general. If leonine, ruthless, and lucky, I should have been by now a full general and candidate for premier. To lack the rank is to lack the qualities. It is as simple as that. The peculiarities of the American system are no excuse. She admired Kennedy, but suspects him of trying to poison his cabinet.

Tonight at the library I read the *Army Times* to see if another promotion is possible. I concluded that it is only a matter of setting it in motion through the proper channels.

I also counted money. A very impressive sum is building up in my savings account, enough to release me from dependence on relatives. If I can take the school for a small ride, I will be able to live very well indeed. Go-to-hell dollars, the dearest money in the world! At the same time I made a note to prepare a will and take full coverage under GI insurance. I know the life insurance idea is laughable, but it's cheap enough I can't resist. M. can be the beneficiary; his life is burdened with people who need a go-to-hell.

I have advanced to the client's chair across from Lwan. I am talking to her in French—so as not to be eavesdropped upon, I tell her. She is puzzled and somewhat infatuated. I am also explaining the Hemingway novels, sentence by sentence. In the interest of purifying reading matter for our boys, I have stolen the Gide. Such things must be reserved to minds which can understand and not succumb.

The commander in chief of assistance forces paid a visit today. It is being bandied about that American troops may soon be brought in force to supplement the locals and advisers. Supposedly, that was the purpose of his visit.

I spent the morning raking leaves, sweeping them into piles, and ordering natives to haul them off and burn them. It reminded me of boyhood daydreams, the yard a nation, the leaves soldiers, and the piles citadels of last resort. Napoleon, Caesar, Alexander, the generals at work. Around noon a native battalion appeared, wearing fatigues and red tunics. There was a striking contrast of bright red and the dull green uniforms. The helmets rocked back and forth on their heads like buckets, accentuated by a devil-may-care attitude; a parade, a vacation! They refused absolutely to stay in step, and once inside the compound sat down in the shade, littering where we had swept.

The necessary rituals, my father used to say. He was offshore for the Philippine invasions, where the officers' beer wagon hit the beach before aid or support artillery. A hell of a hard war, but the only way to fight one. Or so he liked to say. In the absence of today's battalion, two villages were overrun.

The general sprang from the second of a convoy of jeeps and greeted our brigadier. The hair of his crew cut stood so straight that for a moment I thought it must be plastic. With arm in sling—the men call him Old Broken Arm since he received the wound at the Cercle Sportif—he is the figure one sees running around a track in the early morning. The one who wears colored socks with tennis shoes. He interviewed a dozen soldiers in the first line. As they told him name and hometown, he cocked his head and assumed an expression which said that the man's place of birth was perfectly acceptable. As he shook hands around the yard, an undersized brass band, worse than none at all, took its position and prepared to play.

Four times they played ruffles and flourishes, once for each star. The stars were in a straight line on his cap, and I observed that only one or two more, and the dignity would dissolve; the cap would look like a chorus girl's. At each blast, the colors were dipped to his salute. Not that flags mean anything to me, but just this once the thought of lowering the flag stuck in my craw. I cleared my throat and spat.

"You've got the worst sense of timing I ever saw," said Mooney. The pop of mucus had rent a sacred hush. Just then the band struck up the national anthem, and Mooney had to leave off to brace and salute.

After the ceremony the commander stopped in the yard for a television interview. He was standing between the camera and an air conditioner. An aide rushed up to maneuver him to another setting.

Late in the afternoon I was called for another talk by Colonel Y. Mooney has been informing him that my interest in my work is not what it should be; not to mention, I have a tendency to insubordination. It is not an earth-shaking matter, merely an inability to show the maturity my rank requires. Mooney would like to see me reduced. Y. is too near the end of his tour to reduce anyone. Probably nothing would come of it, he reasons, but it might conceivably lead to controversy. However, I am warned.

Mooney gripes that Y. is "no solder," and waits for a certain Colonel Rachow to replace him. Rachow will set things right. Meanwhile, Mooney must endure both the country and his clerk.

Besides hating the country, Mooney misses his wife and children. He speaks of them frequently, apropos of nothing. It is apparent that he takes familiarity for granted even among enemies. He showed me their pictures. He has adopted children as ugly as himself. Red, thick-bodied, weak around the eyes they seem to have just been in an overchlorinated pool. He and his wife can't make it together, he says. This turn in familiarity makes me shudder. There is some sort of infirmity, but I can't make out his meaning. I can't make out whether the doctor believes it to be him, his wife, or both. The problem is in his language. And as little as I like him, I feel it would be unpardonable to probe for what he means.

★ ten ★

ANOTHER DENTAL APPOINTMENT: dentist and drill this time, but also solicitude and cunning caresses from the assistant. If they are meant as caresses at all. She certainly approves of my program. A lovely mouth I have. The dentist agrees. It is called class-one occlusion, he says. Meaning that the upper and lower jaws are a good fit. Dental chair talk puts me in something of a daze. For a while I was unsure in what country I would find myself when I got up. Miss, this is . . .? Just the question we need to ask. And the one that is universally ridiculous. To those who know.

Mooney harps now on the coming of Rachow. The man has supposedly busted a full half of the enlisted men in his aviation battalion. Yes, aviation. He is a helicopter pilot, of all things. "I've got you now, boysan!" says Mooney with knowing eyes. Moreover, he could inform me that Colonel Y. wanted to see me. His face was exceptionally smug.

It had come to Y.'s attention that I have been seeing a native librarian. Officers have been by to discuss it with him. Some of the men feel that I am disrupting her work. In addition, I seem to be getting involved. Recall the law of conquistadors: thou shalt not screw, defecate, or bleed. The Spaniards weighted the body of Cortés with stone and dropped it into the river. At midnight. People who would rule do not die; they feel themselves becoming gods.

Y. reminded me of the free condoms in the orderly room. Responsible men will use the women allocated to that purpose. Mooney stood smiling in the door. He has struck an alliance with a Lieutenant Colonel Nash, who wishes Lwan reserved to himself. The library is proscribed by orders of Colonel Y.

Caesar and the pirates. Who can believe him in his twenties, without legions? Threats taken as jokes. Ransom doubled. Popular, even, among his captors. But they will learn. In good time, shorter than they think, he will return to hang them.

I plot revenge. It pains me to think of M. M. and I are a political entity. But a volatile one. Our friendship is an ad hoc coalition. We hate the same people. M. disapproves my methods. Historical determinism boys don't like it if you are content to kick in a face here and there. I tell him the triumph of the masses is doing little to redress my personal grievances.

It was in basic training, and they stood me in front of the formation. Why did I refuse to go to chapel? No, not a Jew, don't bug me on Saturdays either. A nonbeliever absolute. Don't argue theology, captain, you're out of your province and out of your class. So off I went to the kitchen to wash pots and pans.

That evening the Defender of God, a bulky private, sat at my table. No one, he claimed, had the right not to believe. I must undergo conversion by force. He outweighed me forty pounds.

After dinner I perched on the fire escape and waited. When he approached, I dropped on his back. The weight pulled his shoulder out of socket. Calling up gangster movies, I pummeled the weak underbelly, hitting down like a thug instead of up like a cowboy. A circle formed to watch. I pinned him against the door and hit and kicked him beyond the other fellows' concept of the reasonable. One of them, his pupils dilated, tried to pull me away. I had hit first from behind, he said. I was in luck: the dissenter was small; I flattened him with one lick and returned to belabor the Defender. "Where's your God, where's your God?" I taunted. I spat in his face. Then I made the others carry him to his bunk. That night he spat blood. When he couldn't muster, they made him start over at the first week of training.

Despite all efforts by command, church attendance in the company began to fall off. As the story made the rounds of the barracks, there was a virtual boycott of the Defender's God. In a sense, I suppose, he was proved theoretically sound in trusting conversion by the sword. M. refuses to laugh when I tell this story, but I can tell that it gratifies him enormously.

"Your hat, ass, you hat!"
Several times daily Mooney says it. Its application rests on my being in his power. I feel like pointing out that I am the superior animal, and thus have no reason for taking orders. But it is not precisely true. Things may be done to me. I am vulnerable to commands. Therefore I search for arenas in which my superior strength applies. When I find one . . . Let it at least be said that it was he who initially based matters on force.

An ally: the first sergeant, a decent man, an islander seeking citizenship, a man never fully assimilated to a system of military discipline, though he serves it well enough. He is under pressure himself. I cemented the alliance by taking him to dinner. There is a small restaurant in town, once frequented by the French, where one can assemble a Parisian dinner. There was vichysoisse of good consistency and then crabs amandine, sautéed perfectly, over which to drive a bargain. He was as delighted with being there as with the food; it constituted a sort of lesson in restaurant procedure. The red-and-white-checkered tablecloths and indirect lamps lent a proper atmosphere, a French provincial. Without sinking to feigned democracy or bonhomie, I acquainted the top kick with the irony and misfortune of my situation. And with my future coming-into-my-own.

Since he shared the bond of seeing the army entirely as a vehicle, he could readily understand. I encouraged him to enjoy the wine. He assured me of the first available private room. Thanks, I told him, but the creature comforts mean nothing to me. For my peculiar aims, what I most needed was combat duty. For that, I needed another promotion. Then who could say? Pehaps, returning as a hero, I could serve my country in even higher capacity. *Noblesse oblige*, it says on the family arms. With this combination of patriotism and ambition he was wholly sympathetic. He asked only that I find an hour a week to tutor him in correspondence courses.

His role in the plan was to roster the promotion list by sections. We'll use the army's love of charts and graphs for poetic justice' sake, I said. He must entitle the promotion list as the "Personnel Advancement Effectiveness Report," a command yardstick. It was my theory that if a commander was gauged by the number of his cohorts with drippy penises, he could damn well be measured by how many of his men got promoted. His part would be easy enough, the top said. On the matter of arranging me a private room, he would not take no for an answer.

Mooney returned with the monthly promotions wearing his best Irish-red spluttering look, the look of laughing, crying, swearing, and having a difficult bowel movement all at once.

"Get out the regs, boysan. You will: submit each man for promotion, now and in future months, even yourself. The colonel says. Some goddamn new report has made as ass out of us."

Each night I checked the *Army Times* to make absolutely certain that I, and no one else, was eligible.

There is a day set aside by the natives strictly for undeserved awards. We mock their inscrutable ways, but in this they are straightforward. In our army, routine awards have punctured the words *distinguished* and *meritorious* until the original denotation leaked out. In fact, in our entire military language excellence has leaked from adjectives until few have anything left in them but *passable, acceptable, mediocre*. The Viets make no bones about it. They do not blink at spurious awards. In a calculated defense of their native tongue, they set aside a day each year for the undistinguished. For that day normal significations are suspended. Each man is given accolades. Men lie by prearrangement, so that the words themselves may survive. An April Fool, of sorts. It adds a touch of color to the Class A uniform, while deceiving no one.

Guadette was among the advisers slated to receive awards. He is the replacement for Major DeL., and has been at the corps only a few weeks. In the excitement, I slipped away to the other compound and purchased a bottle of Scotch. I hurried back and confronted a native captain from our counter part section. The bottle went into his desk and we struck up a conversation. Both small-town boys, little provided and much expected, we had common grounds. He had failed of promotion through an insufficiency of funds. The colonels pocketed his bribes without taking the agreed action. A bitter man, he found Scotch to be just the thing—that and an occasional gew-gaw from the PX. In the absence of the reality, we agreed, the appearance is always next best. A paean emerged in rough draft, myself as *dedicated, professional, distinguished*. I asked that he delete *professional*, as the word had an unpleasant connotation for me personally. He gave the paper to his clerk; I would be recommended for the National Medal, the first junior man in the corps so honored. Almost apologetically, he noted that my award would be presented on an ordinary day. The general would pin it on.

As I left his office, there was a commotion in the courtyard. The ceremonies had dragged through the hours of overhead sun, and Major Gaudette, inadequately acclimated, had fainted.

I pointed out to Mooney that since the office was up to strength, there was no cogent reason for not releasing me. That was true, he admitted, but could I demonstrate my fitness for combat? In the first place, he held that men who wanted to go were never fit. Furthermore, I had now been a clerk for . . .

I challenged him to match skill for skill. His uniform, I said, showed no evidence of wartime duty. Did *he* not regret a career of letting other men do the fighting? Let me show him, then he must let me go. He rejoined with tales of serving in the artillery, which was never ballyhooed with medals like the infantry. He had forgotten, he said, more than I knew.

The sergeant major listened. Mooney and I contrived a contest of naming weapons. A verbal duel, the rules: each man to name muzzle velocity, weight, length, rate of fire, and deployment on weapons the other named, turnabout. We matched on fieldpieces. He had indeed spent time in the artillery, but I remain doubtful of his combat experience. Again we matched on the forty-five; the M-79; the seventy-five; the grease gun. More than a verbal contest is required, I thought. I saw images of dueling across a practice range with antitank guns. "Back to back, gentlemen, take four hundred paces, wheel, and fire your rockets. One, two, three . . ."

Then he stumbled. The armalite ninety, he swore, could not be. Two men were required to carry and fire the seventy-five. A ninety held by one man? He would sink in the ground!

I even told him that it was made of aluminum. He either disbelieved aluminum barrels or was too excited to listen. It was an altogether fitting weapon. First, because I had helped test it when it first came out. My expertise did not come entirely from books. Mastering the intricate sight, I had smashed dummy tanks at a thousand yards. Then again, compared to the heavier bazookas, it brought to mind a favorite line from Sherlock Holmes. The wiry little logician is straightening out a poker which has just been bent by a sinister giant. "I am not so bulky," he says.

Mooney was willing to bet a hundred dollars against the weapon's existence. The sergeant major took a side bet of ten. I dictated a generous burden of proof, which the bartender copied and notarized.

The general's manual proved each point of fact. The sergeant major had come in twice, and Mooney had been boasting for the better part of a day as to how he intended to spend the money. I showed him the manual and went over the bet point by point. Payable on payday, I said.

Fuming Irish red, he swore that he had been like a father to me, and I had taken advantage. When he was drunk, no less. Like the cursed son of Noah. My generation had no respect. We would reap our due.

Very well, I said, as long as he paid. He refuses categorically.

★ eleven ★

THE MATTER OF HATS is coming to the crisis. Mooney says that I must wear one when out of doors. Or else. It is a universal principle. It is true anywhere the army goes.

I assure him that I understand, but that the author of this principle did not comprehend its consequences for those with egg-shaped heads. Not that I am good-looking, but I see no cause to look worse than I must. I add, without great emphasis, that hat-wearing is not hygienic in tropical climes. It is a nuisance to boot, and—I admit it—I am absent-minded.

All this makes no dent on Mooney. It is a matter of authority versus insolence. It is a matter of principle: whether or not he can work his way over me. He is, after all, an SFC with eighteen years in. I must admit that there is something of a principle on my side too. I cannot refuse his orders. Instead I make a point of carrying the hat in my belt and compelling him to issue a formal command.

He has asked Colonel Y. to administer discipline. Y. has, of course, refused. He is leaving soon and wishes to sidestep controversy. Nevertheless, he agreed to have the hat rule promulgated as an office regulation. The order was dropped on my desk for typing. Now copies are posted on every wall in the office.

My anger at this strikes me as inhuman. It is as if my mind were a computer, which for the frustration of a tiny subroutine would grow progressively more violent until it unleased destruction of the world. I am a literal Doomsday machine when it comes to orders. What does this remind me of? *If a single idea be destroyed, per impossible, the universe goes tumbling to chaos.* A German?

I bide my time.

There are others here who feel a measure of trickery and a measure of patience go before success. Major Gaudette sits daily at his desk in the hope that the god of paperheaps, his patron, will observe his courage, see him to be a lion, and, in due time, promote him. This is the major's first tour in a combat zone. He jumps out of his chair at the report of artillery. Each time he must be reassured that it is a friendly battery on the edge of town.

Today a case history: Eisenhower, he asserted, stagnated for a decade until the war. Then at once the nation saw a need for steady hands and promoted him over the heads of the fighters. Hands were shaken, smiles smiled, directives phraseologized and promulgated. From light colonel to demigod without intermediate steps. The god of officework cares for his own. Stands at their side making them goodlier, kindlier, and luckier, and bringing well-deserved rewards. Anyone, said Gaudette, can stalk the boondocks with radio and rifle.

Whenever I see Gaudette I rush up to deliver a salute. It has caught on with the men, who will walk twenty yards out of their way to whip one on him. The salutes are not slovenly enough for reprimand, but full of connotation. Like cruel children making goathorns at the town cuckold, we pursue him.

Ike, he kept repeating today, Ike. Great, great

71

Eisenhower! The guns fired a volley and he dropped to the floor.

My promotion is going through. I have spoken with the personnel chief. To become a sergeant is requiring an intrigue. In forwarding the papers, the personnel chief must specify "hard" rank. Otherwise I would be promoted as a clerk.

At first I could not expect the personnel chief to be as accommodating as top. But rumors served well. His staff is of a remarkably consistent physical type. The sergeant major considers the whole thing obscene. They are closeknit and clannish on duty and off. Sergeant major fumes, but no one casts overt aspersions. A master sergeant with sixteen years in! No matter how he rolls his eyes . . .

After dinner, knocking at his door, I was invited in and asked to sit on the bed while he changed clothes. He faced nothing directly, people or business. He looked sideways with darting eyes, eyes that could not be fixed, and his smile, constant in shape, took on varying innuendoes beneath them. With delicacy I talked and listened. I am a progressive. I am no barbarian. I know that Caesar slept not only with his rivals' wives but with houseboys. I am broad-minded. I see little difference, if any, between a man and an ugly woman. Flirtation is the same. The whole process seemed little different than dinner with the top kick. Ends are ends and means are means. Besides, if it should come to an unaesthetic pass, I had the advantage of living fifteen layers deep beneath my skin. He wondered, "But why, for pit-ty's sake, in a combat arm? I'd promote you twice. But where you'd be safe. In the warm bosom of G-1. With me."

I told him that it was the women. I'm one hell of a woman-screwer when I'm back home, I said. A war record would save time and breath. Medals, wounds —nothing I know of is so effective in allaying schoolgirl qualms. And dilatory female tactics. The sexual aura of the man of violence!

At this he was quite taken aback.

"For a finky broad?"

I was reminded of an expedition we made in college. It was Mardi Gras week, and we all left for New Orleans. Between us was only bus fare and five or ten dollars. We'll get all we need by rolling queers, we said. It was a childish boast, one on which nobody intended to make good, but suddenly we were there, without funds, each goaded by the others. We sought out the bars and picked out our marks. For safety's sake, we acted collectively. We didn't beat them unless we had to, simply took the money and ran. Perhaps the ones we beat got the value they desired.

When Mooney heard about the promotion, he assured me that it meant nothing, except that Rachow would have to bust me twice as far. He subjected the personnel chief to bad usage.

Now that the sessions with Lwan are off limits, my evenings have become modestly ascetic. I do exercises and go for conditioning runs. It's as though I were a penitent. Sometimes, with a rifle at port arms, I go for a search and destroy mission on the outskirts of town. Each time I explore a new little area. The search has turned up nothing in the way of enemy. On my deepest penetration I did not turn up so much as a challenge from friendly guards. Still, I intend to continue until I have searched the area within range. Before curfew I must be back in the compound. I read books, and in a sense, meditate. I send E. variations on her form letter.

Last night Colonel Y. asked me to stay late. He had personal correspondence to wrap up and a final report on his accomplishments. His report contained twenty-seven errors: nine comma splices, three split infinitives, six pronouns out of case, two dangling participles, five misspellings, error in subject-verb agreement, and recurring shift of tense. I typed the draft as it stood. A mosquito bit the back of my neck as I was finishing, and I chased it with mosquito bomb until a direct hit knocked it out of the air. As I locked the office of a pang of conscience overtook me. What must a man defend if not his language? I reopened the office, swore, sprayed, and typed again. Y. will not notice. No one will. Language is pure egotism. Those who use it well think nothing of it. Those who don't can't tell the difference. Even M. thinks the love of good speech preposterous. He calls me the neoclassical man.

I jogged to the compound, a distance of two miles. The air was exhilarating, as was the route we travel in the mornings. Gaudette has had me arm and sandbag the jeep. I took a short cut through a patch of cane trees. The run had to suffice as exercise. There would be no time for my search mission.

Once inside the compound, I continued to walk. As the sweat dried, I savored my bitterness as a gourmet enjoys game. Others had made a separate peace; I had to find a separate war.

I walked by the clubs set up for the diversion of the troops. None of the games appealed to me. I looked into the enlisted bar, where Mooney was putting finishing touches on the night. Ending up at the swimming pool, I enjoyed its desertion. Except for occasional enlisted emigrations lasting only a week or two, the pool in daytime is unofficial property of the officers. It is pungent with chlorine—a lieutenant is appointed to make periodic tests. At night the surface

74

looks like a battlefield at the day's end, littered with small creatures floating belly up. Across the pool I could see inside the officers' club where Colonel Y., stripped to his undershirt, was putting a last touch on his own going-away party. A drink settled by his head, he was lying face up on a ping-pong table. His legs dangled off the edge. Without taking my eyes away from the scene, I urinated in the pool.

☆ *part two* ☆

★ twelve ★

Rachow dropped in to inspect the office, and Mooney led him around like a fight manager his gorilla. Another dinosaur.

This one had the large head and thin, agile body of Tyrannosaurus Rex. The head had a shock of white swept-back hair, and there was a white mustache. Slashes with its tail, I mused. A flesh eater, and knows it. The appearance is deceptive. A cousin to the Brontosaurus. Mooney heaved relief at that. But the profile! Teeth in view extending backward to the ears. Tearing teeth. Incisors.

After ten minutes Rachow left. He slashed out the door. The memoranda left for typing were in perfect English.

He did not reappear for two days. When he called me into his office, he insisted that Mooney leave and shut the door. We began with a discussion of my background. Then, quite suddenly, he sat back in his swivel chair and inquired if I was to be trusted. Could I be discreet? I almost burst into laughter at the hint of secret agents and hocus-pocus. The proper responses were slowly winding to the surface when I, quite suddenly and for no reason, told the truth. To the root of things, I said. In that case, I am to be relied upon as much as anyone. A political adage, let us say: if bought, it is wise to stay bought! Hardly a Roman ideal, but appropriate enough for our times. I tried to cover myself with a chuckle. But emotional, blind loyalty? No. He knew my IQ score, from the personnel file, and needn't have asked.

He blinked at my way of putting it, but nodded.

Certain that it was again safe to frequent the library, I had to make a strategic decision: to inform Lwan or not. I decided not. After all, what action is possible in a library? I suggested that we meet at a public place or at her home, for starters perhaps the French restaurant.

That was out of the question, her note replied. A public place was impossible. The police would consider her a businesswoman and make her purchase a card. She had no money for the bribes. We exchanged more notes. She agreed to meet me at her house.

The address she gave brought me before a narrow storefront, not ten meters wide. The wooden floor was covered with finely powdered dirt. Articles for sale were stacked to the height of my shoulders. The bulk of the space was occupied by wooden folding chairs with unfinished surfaces. The walls were lined with children's toys and devices for which I could see no purpose. Perhaps there were toys as well. Just down the street I had seen a child playing with two sticks. The large stick flipped the smaller one, which was more of a chip, end over end into the air. No effort was made to catch it. What impressed me about the sticks was the fine quality of wood and smoothness of their finish. The workmanship far outweighed the ingenuity of the game.

To enter the store, I had to clear a path by pushing aside merchandise. No one was minding it, apparently. Then at the back I saw a doorless opening, behind which Lwan was sitting on a cushion, smiling. She had seen me all along, had noticed my hesitation and rechecking of the address.

I smiled and said hello. This was her mother's store, she said, and they lived upstairs. Her mother appeared from a room still further back. She spoke to me and walked on, without expression, as though she had to tend a customer. I watched her walk out to a makeshift counter, composed of crates covered with a cloth. She stood and stared out the front. No customer appeared. I suggested to Lwan that we go upstairs in order to have more privacy for the English lesson. Drawing the book from under my arm, I waved it back and forth, like an adult enticing an infant to play.

On my third visit she accepted my suggestion that we move upstairs. She made no effort to stop my stealthy touches. Yet I could not seem to get her attention. I felt like shouting, "Look here, pay some attention to what I am doing!" Of course, one must attract attention gradually. I tried to kiss her, but she turned her head from side to side. She reminded me that we were studying English. She is manipulating me, I thought, and bit my lip. Quickly I rearranged my face so she would not notice my impatience. Nothing is so inimical to sex as impatience.

On the way home I walked around the block. I countered twenty small stores before turning the first corner. The miniaturization was striking and deceptive. Did each store, with its small opening, go on forever into the bowels of the city? I assured myself that Lwan's store was indeed limited. There was a bakery on the other side.

On my fifth visit, without prior sign of softening, she submitted to my embrace. I must admit to being

81

startled at the suddenness, being accustomed to seeing women come apart bit by bit. I had a method. The tradition of the lifted siege. The Trojan horse. *I am going away, now, and you have won. Accept this offering in token of your victory.* My cleverness had never failed. It is a matter of patience and control.

In this case, I had seen no prior weakening. I had not begun to stress the triumph of her virtue. As soon as our faces touched, her mouth opened wide and she began to draw as if I were a citrus fruit. She kissed with a rhythmic pulling. It seemed that she was drawing me inside her. I could not believe that she had not kissed this way before.

I moved to exploit my advantage. My hands made a flanking pincer, one on the leg, one on the back. As they met, she recoiled and pushed them away. In doing so, she did not even break the rhythm of her kiss.

On the next visit I picked her up and walked around the room with her, hoping that the ride might jolt her into involuntary action. She asked me not to take her near the small balcony where we might be seen. As I brought her back from view, we passed a dresser on which there was a sitting Buddha about eighteen inches high. As I turned to look at it, she began to writhe in my arms and insisted that I put her down. Her Buddha must not see her in such condition.

Later in the evening she made another surrender, but insisted on interruption to prevent pregnancy.

I decided to make small talk as is always done. I noted that her skin was not yellow at all. It was in fact lighter than mine. I explained that the books I read as a child showed Orientals with yellow faces. She said that she was indeed white, and had never thought of herself as a yellow person.

I noticed too that her features were somewhat different from those of the typical Vietnamese. She said that this was because her father was Chinese. That also accounted for her height, she said, and for her quick mind and curiosity. I persisted in this line of questioning. Her mother is the second of her father's two extant wives. The father set her up in business, but does not live with her. He visits frequently, but must do his first wife the honor of living with her. He is a rice merchant. The Chinese are always merchants. They go all over the world and make money because they are intelligent and conniving. Sometimes the people turn on them and kill them. The people of Vietnam are very hostile to the Chinese, although some, like her mother, marry them. Her mother is very unhappy, and thinks that all men are evil. I asked Lwan if she had ever heard of Jews, and she said no.

Her father is a cruel man, and she hates him. He is irresponsible and never does anything for his children. A moment later, she says he is clever and she admires him very much. I asked her which was the true opinion, and she could not say. He had forced her to learn French, Chinese, and English. Her mother speaks only Vietnamese, and has trouble telling Americans how much to pay. Her father made Lwan learn the classics. That was the way with Chinese. In one of them, she said, a Chinese dreamed he was a butterfly, and when he woke up, he thought perhaps he was a butterfly who had dreamed he was a man.

Chuang-Tzu, I said. She could not recall the name herself, but was fairly certain that whatever I had said was not it. How would I know? Anyway, it didn't matter who had said it.

★ thirteen ★

THE ROOM is now all mine. A few days ago, the top kick called me aside to say that at T.'s department I would have it to myself. He had managed to juggle the books so that a man under token assignment to the unit is to be my official roommate. The man is on permanent "temporary duty" elsewhere.

For weeks T. had been celebrating his departure. Like mine, it will coincide with discharge from the army. In honor of this fact, he replaced his name tape with the initials F.T.A. He says I may guess the signification although he intends to tell superiors that it stands for Future Teachers of America. His last weekend, extended by a day on each side, was spent downtown. He returned boasting that he had "gotten" ten more, one of them a cherry girl. It had cost fifty-two dollars. The FUCK COMMUNISM sign was taken down and packed as a souvenir. He said that he sincerely hopes his mother will not run across it in his things. He showed me another souvenir, a jacket bought in Saigon, made of cheap black leather with a gold map of Vietnam on the back. Engraved on the map are the words, I KNOW I'LL GET TO HEAVEN CAUSE I'VE SERVED MY TIME IN HELL! Beneath, in slightly different lettering are the date, the locale, and T.'s name. T. mentioned that the dates of his tour are off by one month, but that no one would know the difference.

Saying that I seemed to have a good deal of savoir for my years, he asked me to help him select gifts for "some buddies and some womenfolks." One day at lunch he came over and I accompanied him downtown. After an hour and a half of touring shops, we had pretty well covered the local market. Besides a variety of merchandise made from military surplus there were combs and charms in the shape of Chinese writing, wooden plates with mother-of-pearl, and objects made of buffalo horn. Oddly the objects were almost exactly what I would have imagined. T. was fascinated with the charms. They had Chinese letters symbolizing wealth, love, and longevity. I steered him toward the objects with more valuable material, and left him to his own taste. I recommended that he eschew brass, and look twice at items which seemed to be sold on a basis of workmanship. Buy melt-down value, I enjoined. He thanked me, but was reticent about displaying the final choices.

Toward the end, the word hello was replaced in his vocabulary by greetings such as, "Nine more and fuck 'em, buddy!"

At the end of the day Mooney asked me to have a drink at the club. It would be incongruous, I said, since he had just spent the day boasting how he and Rachow were going to have me busted. He said not at all, that his desire to see me knocked down a peg was purely professional. His desire to drink with me was personal.

"You don't like me, do you?" Mooney asked. "You don't like the kind of person I am."

During the afternoon I had filed a formal request for transfer. Mooney assured me that it would be turned down, but I insisted that it be processed. Then

I filed another request, asking that my tour be short-ened. I had found it in regulations. *Any person duly enrolled in an institution of higher learning, and eligible for registration . . .*

They would be good enough to return me a few weeks early so as to prepare for school. I do not mean "Good enough." I mean that it is in their regulations, and at this point they have no choice.

"You really hate me, don't you? You think you're too fine to be associating. You think you're too good for us, don't you?"

Mooney was quick to note that I was asking for a new assignment on the one hand, while on the other I was asking early leave. If I received the new as-signment, it would make no sense for the army to train me in a new set of duties only to have me pick up and leave in a month or two. Was that not correct? Absolutely, I said. Then we'll return this application to you at your own request. We would do no such thing, I said. He spent over an hour looking through regs, but did not find a rule to back his view. Both requests were passed to personnel.

"Well you're a sergeant yourself now, isn't that right?"

But I wouldn't be one for long. He'd make sure of that. Just as soon as he could get that new colonel un-tracked and down to business in the office. He'd make a soldier out of me. There were things to be done to him also, I said.

"What would you like to do with me?"

"Shoot you," I said.

"Are you threatening a noncommissioned officer?"

"No. I said '*like* to shoot you.' I didn't say I would."

"It's the same thing."

"Not at all. If I shot you I'd have to pay the price. I am clearly not going to, because I am unwilling to

86

pay. I inform you of that forthwith. In no way am I obligated to stop wanting to."

"I could have you tried for threatening a noncommissioned officer."

"It won't stand up in court. Not even a military court."

Late in the afternoon he asked me again to have a friendly drink with him. I declined.

I myself have purchased a couple of native objects as souvenirs. While advising T., I noticed a pair of long-necked birds carved from the horns of water buffaloes. They were just the kind that old ladies are ecstatic to receive. They cost a thousand piasters—ten dollars, more or less, depending on whether one uses the official rate or the going market. I probed my memory for an old lady on whom to bestow them. Failing of recollection, I assured myself that eventually there would be such an old lady in my life. Perhaps the mother of a future wife. They would have been saved just for her. I pictured them decorating a living room mantel. I even envisioned the furniture, the lamp shades, and floor-length drapes.

A buffalo herd leaves piles right in the center of town. It gives the city a touch of authenticity, I think, not only that they are water buffalo instead of cattle, but that they are accepted as a matter of course in the square. They recall a story I was told by a veteran of the last war. With a squad of MPs on patrol outside Manila, he had come across a water buffalo, an old cow, drinking at a stream. One of the younger men, impatient with unexciting duty, drew a bead and shot her in the flank. She had received a mortal wound, and there was nothing to be done at that point. The men simply stood around to watch her die. She stumbled slowly to her knees. Then an idea began

87

with an absurd boast, grew to a dare, and then to a bet. The man who had shot her was dispatched to her haunches to pull the buttocks apart. One by one the men approached and mounted her. The man who told the story believed—though no one could be sure— that he had been the one upon her when she died.

★ fourteen ★

THE ARMY has returned an affirmative answer on my request for an early discharge. Mooney can hardly believe it. He is wroth, but impotent under the circumstances. I tell him that it is simple enough, that they were clearly obligated.

Major Gaudette is honing the masterwork of his career, a campaign plan for the dry season. Although I am doing his typing, I have been unable to tell for sure whether it pertains to the dry season now under way or the one that will come at this time next year. He himself may not know for sure the precise intent of his orders, and so be leaving it purposefully vague.

In general, he is not a hard person to work with. Of late, he suspects that Rachow disapproves of him, and is consequently irritable, but otherwise he takes things well. It is patently unfair, he insists, to look with condescension on a man who has not seen combat, so clearly unfair that Gaudette does not intend to let it worry him. He now speaks of retirement to Florida. One more promotion, he says, will be sufficient. He no longer seeks to rally his career like Eisenhower. There is really little difference, he stresses, between a lieutenant colonel and a colonel. In a neighborhood of retired businessmen, one is referred to without the modifier.

His campaign plan is designed to work through subcontracts. First Gaudette sends requests to the division headquarters. The general, he tells them, requests their submission of a plan in their area of responsibility. Then to parallel staff sections: would they please prepare a plan in their field of competency? These are signed under a stamp which reads FOR THE COMMANDER.

At first I imagined that the system placed an unfair burden on the subordinates, but when the reports began to arrive, I realized that these had been able to pass the requests to still lower levels. In the end no one was burdened with more than he could bear. The final plan will consist of collated fragments, so small that it is difficult to trace individual origin.

I cannot help thinking of storybook complaints from soldiers made to carry out details. There comes to mind an engineer ordered to blow a strategic bridge, and his tenacious fidelity of execution, his death, for an attack that never came off. It is to be granted that our system avoids such incidents.

For weeks Gaudette has been assembling fragments and having me type them into a consistent prose and format. Each morning he brings battle gear to the office, and in midmorning leaves for a helicopter which has been put at his disposal. He has instructed me to keep records of the flight data. My attention has been drawn to the fact that a hundred flying hours qualifies one for an Air Medal. This requirement is reduced by half if the flight is considered combat support, and by half again if it is classified direct assault.

Gaudette has consulted me in classifying flights, and a Newtonian principle has evolved. It is a matter of thinking gradually, in small finite steps. At the outset we agreed that his flights were strictly administrative.

At no point has this statement been flatly contradicted. On the other hand he has taken along battle gear, weapon included, and perhaps the word "strictly" was injudiciously chosen. While the flights have been "administrative" in some respects, in others they are indistinguishable from combat support. It is a matter of the jurisdiction of words. One may assign the words "combat support" a wide or narrow construction. It is even arguable that all flights are combat support. For that matter, I pointed out, one might say that flights of airlines in the states have a certain resultant as "combat support." But in that event, there would be no rationale for the category "administrative" at all. "That will do, young man," said Gaudette. In the end it was settled that his flights were rather to the "support" side of any imaginary line one might draw. A few days later the process began again. This time Gaudette observed that, while he had not discharged his weapons, it was there with him, and he would have done so had the necessity arisen. In this light, the difference between "support" and "direct assault" began to take on a cloudy quality. Again, he has employed the epsilons and deltas, and again they seem to be approaching a limit on the "combat" side of the arbitrary line. He will shortly instruct me to upgrade his record accordingly. Soon he will have the Air Medal. It is to be granted that upon return from a flight, he undergoes facial contortions worthy of a man who has been under fire.

The other reports fall into two categories, Monthly and One-of-a-Kind Reports. On the monthly reports I merely change the names and dates. My premise is that the facts are interchangeable. I have a roster, the names of towns listed as the first sergeant has names on a duty roster. Duc Hoa, Tuy Hoa, My Tho, Dong Tam—each serves its turn. There is one battle a month.

What's the difference if there are two? I have standardized the statistics as well. Ours. Theirs. We lead by a steady three-to-one. Which is good, but not good enough. Any worse and there would be alarm. Any better and the statistics would be checked. No one really reads the reports. I never bother with the facts. When a town comes up on my roster, I put the monthly battle there. That's the way it is with war. Unfortunately, I cannot do the same with One-of-a-Kind Reports. They record singularities, innovative mistakes, windfalls, inventions.

One day I found Rachow leafing through the reports. One-of-a-Kind Reports seemed to amuse him. He brought me a copy of an army manual, CREATIVE LEADERSHIP AND COLLECTIVE TUNNEL VISION, US ARMY TM 52-350. The author was listed as a Lieutenant Colonel Rachow. The explanation went as follows. His graduation paper at Command and General Staff College had been on the subject of "leadership manuals." He had barely gotten the subject allowed; over half the class wrote on Clausewitz and strategy in international game theory, the currently fashionable subject. His basic point had been that leadership could not be taught through manuals; he used the term "collective tunnel vision" to lambast such efforts; he cited the failure of taught leaders in unique situations. The paper made quite a stir, and had him on the verge of being failed in the course. Then it caught the attention of the Chief of Staff.

For two years a panel of senior officers considered its ideas. A unit was set up to perform research. At the end of this period the panel, by majority vote, issued the manual he displayed. There had been no way of keeping his name from being cited, although only one chapter actually reflected his thesis. The rest, for the sake of fairness, offered the opposing view.

The manual noted that "there are those who say leadership cannot be taught through manuals"; this ran counter to the army point-of-view that everything could be done, given a sufficient amount of will. The result was the institution, throughout the army, of One-of-a-Kind Reports, to provide instruction in the hitherto neglected area of unique situations. Rachow had written the Chief of Staff to inform him that the thesis had been turned into a Russellian paradox. As a result, the chief's aide, a colonel, had been detailed for two months to read the complete works of Bertrand Russell.

Rachow asked me if I would mind working late to help him adjust a planning project. I agreed, and he outlined the situation. The Vietnamese commander, a three-star general, long known to be a profiteer, collaborator, and plotter with elements in exile, had lost his immunity through the death of his prominent relative in Saigon. He would shortly be replaced, and with his removal, American troops in regular units would be introduced to the corps for the first time. As far as Rachow knew, no one else had yet realized that this change would require a Joint Command and necessitate a shakeup in the organization chart. There was no reason to let such an opportunity slip by without capitalizing. "After all," he said, "even if we do not have the highest hopes for the purpose and efficacy of a system, it is certainly desirable that those of us who see through things float upward at every opportunity." With that sentiment, I could heartily concur.

We began by facing facts. In the first place, there was no way of supplanting the general. Secondly, Rachow was somewhat down the line among the full colonels in terms of time-in-grade. On an A-frame we put up a series of charts, showing the current organization of the corps. We included the rank and seniority of each officer. Then, as Rachow dictated, I constructed a series of tentative reorganizations. The trick, he said, was to use his present position as logical jumping-off point to a similar position with more embrasive powers.

As he dictated, I managed to keep abreast of his ideas and even to make suggestions. He was not young, around forty-five I guessed, and as the night wore on his face took on the consistency of cookie dough. As he tired, his face became ambivalent. He could have been a swashbuckler engaging in sword duels or a pimp on a dark street. Such was the ambiguous quality of the white mustache and swept-back hair.

Again and again tentative solutions were proposed. He asked my opinion, and time after time one or the other of us found a flaw. Colonel A. is too clearly slighted. The jurisdiction may be eroded in the area of logistics. The placement of Colonel B. is not consistent with the placement of Lieutenant Colonel R. My admiration grew as I watched the tiring colonel fight for domination of his peers. He would have been magnificent, I thought, as a papal lawyer in the twelfth century. Or perhaps as the head of a noble family encroaching on its vassals.

From time to time he stopped for philosophic observations. Although I was not always certain of the balance between irony and seriousness, I felt an understanding growing. He might have made a superb field marshal, he said, just as he might have been a fine French chef. The art is the same. It is a matter of laying out many ingredients in ordered places then turning on the heat. Little by little a document took shape.

One by one his rivals were isolated, pushed aside to inconsequential titles far from the seat of power. In the labyrinth of lines, dotted, crossed, and broken, all roads literally led to Rachow. He called the new position Deputy for Plans and Operations. Suddenly his hand darted to the chart and the one remaining rival, deputy to the general, was stranded in the margin with only administration and protocol to support him.

We've done it, he said. Except that he had to devise a wording that would enable him to invade the general's affairs. He settled for "joint supervisory responsibility, plans and operations, of subordinate units." He'll accept it, said Rachow. He'll have no choice. Not a general alive has actually organized a joint command. None of the other colonels were capable. If they were, it wouldn't matter. It will hit them too suddenly. He will accept this with gratitude and be glad to preside over what is left. In fact, he may find it very comfortable.

Yes, I said to Rachow. It appeared, in a matter of speaking, that he was to be Mayor of the Palace.

On the drive back to the compound we heard a flight of B-52s passing over on their way from Guam. I had never imagined that they would bomb so early in the morning. It was still completely dark. My uncle had bounced me on his knee describing the sound of Lancaster bombers passing over London on the way to Germany. He had been a bomber pilot himself, flying support for Patton. The Lancasters came over, he said, like a woman in labor. They flew single file. They did not specify point targets. The first dropped a flare in the center of town and the others dropped their blockbusters on it. Because of human error, they missed, but a function for random misses assured a pattern of destruction around the square. Pilots were warned against becoming precise in an effort to be heroes. An occasional factory might escape, but the town was certain to receive a mortal wound.

My uncle imitated the sound of returning Lancasters, an effeminate whine. He moved his hands back and forth in front of my face, indicating empty planes in single file. It pained him that his own command had been so fastidious. To hell with bombing factories!

Rachow gave me the day off. I told him I would be happy to work in order to conceal our special project, but he insisted. I went to the guard tower in order to watch the sunrise. The night artillery, with brilliant tracer rounds, was still streaking across the sky. My uncle, I reflected, may well have been right. While the Americans advanced more rapidly, the British were certainly more biblical. Leave not a stone upon another! Perhaps that was the point of it, that in war it is better to be biblical than tactical. The dazzling orange streaks against a predawn sky were from our guns, which fire a nightly barrage of random patterns. They put a random blanket on jungle paths. It is classified as harassment and interdiction. This is total war, I have heard the general say; we did not seek war! The flares too are beautiful, both white and multi-colored, although of somewhat less intensity than fireworks.

There were even a few machine gun trails in the distance, with tracers of red and orange. Far off was a rumbling of explosions, comforting as summer thunder. Good sleeping weather. I watched and watched and asked myself if I had felt a twinge in my tooth. Soon it would be dawn.

★ fifteen ★

JUST WHEN I had forgotten it, my award arrived from Saigon. Rachow summoned me into his office and informed me that I was to be made a hero of the Vietnamese people.

A captain and a lieutenant colonel were to be decorated with me. The colonel had reached the point of his career at which he was due a Legion of Merit, more or less as a Good Conduct Medal given field grade officers. The captain had, at risk of life or injury, stood on a bomb that had been tossed into an ARVN training camp. The bomb did not go off. He was to receive an Honor Medal from the locals and a Bronze Star from his own unit. If the bomb had gone off, he would have received the Cross of Gallantry and at least a Silver Star.

The battalions in green fatigues and red tunics marched into the courtyard. They looked like lackadaisical midgets in the oversized American helmets. But no, it was only that their legs were short. The small brass band was lined up beside the reviewing stand. I could see Mooney watching from behind the wooden shutters of the office. Both generals, ours and the native commander, were walking from their adjacent offices toward the reviewing stand. They did not speak or stop to salute. Although they would speak to each other of us warmly, the little exercise was revealed as a disruptive chore by the impatience of their walk, their late arrival. The band weakly struck up the Star-Spankled Banner, then a march which I presumed to be the national anthem of this country. Messengers walking from office to office with papers in their hands had to drop the papers to their sides, stand fast, and salute with the rest of us. One or two senior officers, even, were caught as passersby, and had to stop. The ARVN captain who had submitted me for decoration was in the forefront of the native formation. He was looking at me and smiling widely beneath his salute. When the music stopped, motion resumed all over the courtyard like a movie reel halted and allowed to turn again. To my disgust, I realized that I had a bit of a lump in my throat and would have to blink back tears.

One way or another the story of my decoration seems to have made the local papers. I vaguely recall being made to fill out a form at the Information Office. It may even have requested the name of my local paper. I am sure, however, that, as a joke, I would have listed the *New York Times*. Perhaps the name of my town was sufficient. It is undeniable that someone furnish the paper with information. Three letters have come already.

One is from the local banker. He has noted the service I am rendering to my country and our way of life. He says that he has now read the Kant I recommended. I suppose I did, at a party sometime around sophomore year, recommend that he read something by Kant. It seemed to me then that he would have to send to Germany for it. I refused to admit the fact that our local library, though small, is quite large enough to contain a few volumes of Kant. The jacket, the title, the words are identical to those found in university libraries, even in Germany itself. He wishes me to know that he is impressed with "that categorical imperative." When I return he wishes to discuss business with me and would not be surprised if the bank had an opening for me somewhat more advanced than that offered the ordinary trainee.

There is also a letter on the letterhead of the local veterans. It is a form letter, but a longer message is written in the margin. In fact, there are four copies of the same letter, inviting me to join the organization, with an extended note in the margin written by a well-known citizen of the town, whose name is familiar to me, but whom I cannot seem to place. There is only one veterans' group in town, although most towns have three. They differ ideologically, one of the right, one of the left, one of the center. Our town, however, must settle for one, just as it makes do with one funeral home. It is a fact stemming from the limited market. There are only two major grocery stores. As the town has something of a conservative character, it is the rightist group which has prevailed. In childhood I read their magazine, which came in the noon mail, during my after-school trip to the toilet. For some reason, I can recall certain letters to the editor. Claiming that the latest national convention has surpassed those in the past, they cite Miami, Denver, or Omaha as the ultimate pleasure-capital for old soldiers.

The author of the note written in the margin suggests that I might wish to begin my membership with a talk to the general assemblage on some facet of the war. After all, I am to be the first representative of this war to return. Only one other member of the community has been here, and he has gotten away to a nearby town, where he works in a mill. He never filled out the membership form. If I desire, the forms may be prepared for me and kept in his desk for my arrival.

Coincidentally, he adds, the timing of my eligibility is fortuitous, for a member has just been lost to old age. A man is named, one of the town's last survivors of the initial world war. Veterans of the first war faded fast, says the writer. He is rather startled by their disappearance. Veterans of the Spanish War and the War Between the States had a way of lingering on and on. One grew accustomed to them and their stories, well into the era of the world wars. Scarcely had the last Spanish survivor passed than it became clear that First War survivors were fading. He sincerely hoped that the same would not hold for the Second and subsequent wars.

The man he mentioned was again familiar, although I had troubles once again with the face. I am sure, however, that I know who he means, a thin old man, who wore suspenders. He was something of a legend in the town. When he returned from the war, he purchased the torso of a mannequin and set it in his living room, dressed in his military coat and hat. It was to preserve the shape of the clothes, he said; he vowed to be buried in them. In his declining years, though I never knew him in any others, he sat on the front porch next to the screen door. He had a flyswatter in his hand from early spring to late fall, and could be seen popping flies which lit on the screen. It was the talk of the town when someone discovered that he baited the inside of the screen with molasses. I even heard it said that as he grew feeble—"my reflects aren't what they used to be" as he put it—he spent hours over a card table with wood, nails, and rubber bands trying to invent an automatic, trigger-operated flyswatter. When he died, the note in the margin confided, his wife made a row about displacing the uniform from its mannequin, and he was buried in a seersucker suit.

The third letter was from my father. It mentions a party already in the works, months early, to celebrate my homecoming. I can anticipate the format.

It will serve as a test of power for the old man, who will watch the prominent men from that part of the state assemble within his walls. The return of a hero being one of the most auspicious occasions there, he will most likely be satisfied with the results. The guests will arrive in three shifts. The early shift will consist of guests with small fanaticisms about liquor or conversation, and of certain obligatory invitations, old friends of his parents no longer taken seriously in the town. The second group will be somewhat more even in sociability. They will be drawn from business associates, mostly close subordinates, and will cut smarter figures in terms of dress and posture. They will arrive at eight. By nine thirty lingerers from the second group will feel more and more out of place as prominent men, the mayor and local politicians, the college president, business superiors, and old friends from around the area begin to filter in. There will be much gaiety, and the best quality of liquor will be set out in the kitchen.

He will ask me to wear my class A uniform with medals. It will be necessary to stand in a receiving line for each set of guests.

I will accept compliments, apologize for allowing myself to become thin, and bask in having a sunburn in the middle of the winter. An old lady or two will point to my medals and comment, my, aren't we proud! She will go on to name two distant cousins who also received medals in the war. She may have the wars confused, but that is no great matter. Perhaps their decorations may be entirely routine. She may even know it. It will be her way of mitigating the oddness that I have been decorated by a foreign government.

My mother's arm will nudge me. "Mrs. C. is speaking to you." I will turn my eyes to the right, and sure enough . . .

Toward the end of the evening, when only men of good will remain, I will be accepted into a sort of circle of survivors. As if performing an initiation rite, one will get up and fix me a drink, and another will insist that I tell stories. I will decline three times, as clamor builds, and launch into my tale. The theme is expected to be the horror of war, the depravity of our enemies, and the ways I escaped and triumphed through no virtue of my own. "There were Indians to the left of me, Indians to the right of me, Indians . . ." All is attributed to divine grace. If I wish to make a lasting impression, I will refer to God, in a slip of the tongue, as The Big Soldier. The minister will mention the possibility of my delivering an inspirational talk at church.

My mother is quite capable of having a WELCOME HERO banner up in the yard. She may not, but she is capable of it.

The letter says—I read this part again to get the words precisely—that "the local Republicans have expressed an interest." It is added, by way of analysis, that the party has had rough sledding in legislative elections, and with authentic heroes in short supply, I might very well be able to secure a nomination to the lower house the next time around. In these matters youth, zeal, and innocence are not liabilities.

★ sixteen ★

ONCE MORE I asked Mooney to let me go. He need
only say the word . . . Wars, he made it absolutely
clear, are reserved to those who do not want to go.

The boy down the block was flipping his wood chip.
The storefront was, as always, deserted. Not a very
thriving business. I wondered if she had to meet overhead, or if her husband had purchased leases and
made a gift of the merchandise. The folding chairs
seemed untouched, as did the toys. It seems that she
had added nothing. Perhaps she had sold one or two
small items. Perhaps the husband had overcalculated
vastly, so vastly that she would be able to live off
capital for the rest of her life, slowly liquidating the
initial stock.

Lwan was not waiting in the back room. Without a
word to me, her mother sent for her. Lwan was angry
when she appeared at the foot of the stairs. She said
that I would have to leave right away. After some exchange, it was agreed that I could stay until she told
her story.

A Lieutenant Colonel Nash had been making im-
proper advances. If I had not noticed, I must have
been blind. His glances had always been obscene. Tonight as closing time approached, he waited until

everyone left the library and stalked her around the room. He maneuvered her against the card catalog. Unable to get a grip on her, he attempted to ravish her through clothes. Though fully protected by her silk trousers and his uniform, she felt herself poked and prodded by his protruding belly. His meager masculinity did not even make a dent. Carried away to the point of recklessness, he attempted to undress himself. At this point, in desperation, she took advantage of his clumsy distraction to push him aside and bolt out the door. Realizing that an appeal for help would cost her job, she hid behind the last row of barracks. Later she had the presence of mind to return and lock up the library. He had left a note asking her to meet him at her home.

In the heated aftermath, it soon became clear, she had decided to consider this indignity a blot on the conscience of mankind, masculine gender. Thus, indirectly, I was implicated.

Returning with Chanel perfume and a portable radio, I became the repository for tears previously held back. Still her face jumped from one expression to the other: insult waiting for a comforter, rage accusing all. I had an inspiration and suggested to her that by *our* plans all thought of lost honor might be removed. I said I had been meaning to tell her for some time. I scarcely had a chance to discuss the idea when she took it up completely.

She had a suitable future already plotted. I would remain in the army, but go to a school to assure myself of a clerical job. If I desired, I might eventually become an officer in a clerical specialty. The war would soon end. With luck, I would be retired by the next one. I noted with grudging admiration that she had finally mastered the essentials of our system. After only twenty years, she said, I could retire on half pay to a little house in Florida.

Our house would be small like the library. The walls would be lined with books. She had even observed my idiosyncrasies and prejudices. I could choose the books carefully over a period of years, avoiding mysteries and Westerns entirely. She would catalog them. We would have two children, a boy and a girl. In the last months of each pregnancy, she would allow me, by Vietnamese custom, to go to businesswomen. As long as I did not do so too often or waste money. She paused, bit her lower lip, as if afraid to tell the last part. She would talk on the telephone whenever she wished, and smile and laugh like an American woman.

I should have been outraged to hear myself described as the homesick soldier ready to bring home a dubious trophy. I felt nothing of the kind. For one thing, the secure knowledge that I had told an effective lie seemed to place me above anger. But it was more than that. For a moment the whole thing did not seem so preposterous at all. What if I were telling the truth? It would be no more than the typical marital disaster, at least if her affection for me was genuine. I wondered. It occurred that I would like to have had an electroencephalograph, a pulse record, a record of her glandular secretions during our conversation.

Of course, the army was already committed to sending me home early, so that I was absolutely safe. Nevertheless, the fleeting conviction that I would do as well to stay and marry her after all invested my telling with reality. Suddenly she was changed again, and now ready, she said, to make love complete-ly.

She released something beneath her hair, revealing a hidden bun, and long black strands tumbled over each other until their tips dusted the small of her back.

I marveled at the resources hidden from my eyes. She stood naked before her dresser, facing her Buddha, and swayed the upper half of her body to toss the hair from side to side. She made it wild and tangled, all the while pretending that she was setting it in order. As I stood behind her, she led my hands from region to region, giving at moments of sensation some gesture to indicate that she had been only protecting her flesh.

The Vietnamese, she told my reflection in her mirror, is sensual and delightful when she grows old. I asked if Miss Chi, her skinny assistant, would grow sensual with age. She pouted and asked why I teased her. Grabbing my wallet, she removed the picture of E. and demanded that I destroy it for her. I ripped it horizontally and vertically, suppressing an impulse to shrug. When I dropped the pieces in the trash basket, Lwan claimed that I would someday do the same to her.

She was standing before a high triangular dresser. It fit tightly into the corner of her room. Somehow I had never noticed it. Surely it was always there. It reminded me of an American antique of the last century. She was staring glassy-eyed as if lost in thought. Her complexion clouded, and her features grew less sharp like those of a woman making love. I looked to the top of the dresser, where she was staring. On top I saw another bolhisattva, in the same pose as her desk-top Buddha, but more likely a piggy bank than an icon. Perhaps the piece itself was not a dresser but some kind of corner cupboard. Its surface was rich and old, but I could not make out the type of wood. After a while Lwan began to reach and slowly came to her tiptoes. It seemed that the little bodhisattva-bank was just outside her grasping radius. Slowly she pressed herself onto her toes, stretching each intermediate muscle from toes to fingertips. The skin of her upper stomach traveled across her diaphragm, up and across her ribs. The outline of ribs rippled past. The navel, first drawn from an ellipse into a circle, began to elongate and flatten. Up went her heels, and I marveled that I could see the tiny increments of lift, each coming when her ability to stretch was seemingly exhausted. Her navel was almost flat, the hole disappearing with pressure from inside, above, and below. Her buttocks tightened. She gave a soft grunt, involuntarily, as if a muscle had been pulled, and hung immobile. She hung as if suspended on a string. I noticed that her finger had just touched the china bank, and was gently rocking it back and forth. Silently, without further pressure, it began to topple end over end. Moving as in a reel played in slow motion, it floated toward the floor. The whole thing was taking minutes, perhaps longer. Still she hung up between ceiling and floor. Turning and turning, the bank approached the floor. Without a sound it exploded against the wood, with fragments scattering in slow motion. Hundreds, thousands of pennies scattered in random waves across the floor. She knelt to pick them up, but as she doubled over, I realized that she was only hiding her nakedness.

I decided to jog to the compound rather than taking a cyclo. As I turned onto the main street, I heard small arms fire a block or two behind me. Perhaps a hotel about to be blown, or a bar where officers relaxed. Quite recently, one of the small hotels in town, in which several Americans resided, had been damaged by satchel charges. First comes the gunfire to distract the guards, then an explosive charge on wheels. In that particular case, the laundry boy is missing and under suspicion. Regulations say to put on a steel helmet and pull your mattress over you, although I never bothered during my stay in Saigon. While I thought of this, I heard the crunch of an explosion. There was not time before curfew to go back and investigate. Besides, the night air, while I ran, was exhilarating. Soon the route home merged with the route we take in the mornings.

"Guerrilla war! That's the trouble with it," said the gate guard. He gestured that I need not show an ID card. Had I heard what happened downtown? Had I perchance just been there? From the facts relayed to him, Charlie had blown a riverside restaurant. The weapons used were claymores, our own surplus. Actually, the charges were aimed at the street corner outside. The first charge cut down three loiterers. The second, timed to go off two minutes later, got fifteen spectators. Americans and local officials, they had rushed out in the middle of their dinners to mill around and watch.

The morning tabloid the next day had a human interest story. An official had been wounded. When he fell, his friend was certain he was a goner. Red stuff spurted from his mouth. It was clam soup.

★ seventeen ★

SPEAKING TO THE DENTIST on my most recent visit, I tried to pin down a fact within his area of expertise. I remembered being told that adults beyond a certain age no longer suffer from deterioration of the teeth. It is possible that I misunderstood or never heard such a statement at all. It might well be wishful thinking. In fact, cases come to my mind which would tend to refute it.

The dentist was noncommittal, even when I explained to him the importance of confirming or refuting this thesis. It has occurred to me that when my chart is covered with slashes I might have false teeth replace the entire content of my mouth. While noncommittal about decay, the dentist was able to say that he believed the government obligated to replace teeth on which it had operated. The adjacent ones also.

I lingered to watch the technician mark my chart. She seemed efficient and hardly in need of checking. As she did not seem busy, I asked if I might look at my records in general. The program is coming along nicely. We leaned forward to inspect the charts, and again she shifted her feet so as to caress me with her breasts, this time brushing my arm. Outside the silk blouse, in the open air, they may be meager, soft, almost mushy. Through the blouse they appear smooth and full of independent life. They seem to be struggling to the surface for air.

The ceiling fan turned slowly.

"This godforsaken country," said Mooney. "God forsook it!"

There was a lizard on the ceiling, just above the blades. I contemplated getting out the insect bomb to spray it, to see what would happen. Somehow the act was gratuitous, and I held back. A few days ago I took out the spray and stood on a chair to bombard the bat which makes a home under the edge of the roof. There was a hidden hole in the stucco material. He sped away like his proverbial cousin, but returned by the next morning.

It dawned on me that I could actually count the rotations of the fan. I began doing so, but realized that I had not checked a clock or any other standard of measure. I cannot even remember the number of revolutions I reached, although it was something over three hundred.

"How about breaking down and going to the club with me, boysan? I'll go you one better. Come downtown and I'll buy you a piece. Make a man out of you."

I counted over a hundred more rotations.

"I guess you're too good for that too? Well let me tell you, boysan, a whore is doing her job like everybody else."

I got up and had a cup of water. I do not drink the office coffee. It is my duty to make it. In the past, the low-ranking man has always bought it. Or else negotiated with the mess sergeant. I refused, and when Mooney asked why, I said right away that I didn't drink it myself and was not of a mind to buy for the office. Now it costs a dime a cup. There is a sign on the empty tin. The officers do not pay. There is a periodic crisis when I make them ante up before replenishing it. Mooney is furious. To save embarrassment, he sometimes pays out of his pocket.

For the last several months I have not boiled the water. There has been an upsurge in minor stomach discomforts, although nothing serious has resulted. I drink only from the water cooler, which I boiled scrupulously. With a cup in my hand, I make a little tour around the office to break the monotony. Major Gaudette has constructed a wall-size map, which is impressive in its use of color, but which confuses the 2d batallion of the 4th regiment wtih the 4th of the 2d. The bat has returned on a permanent basis, and I believe he may even have a mate.

★ eighteen ★

ON SUNDAY MORNING the CQ runner appeared at my door and told me to dress and report. A member of headquarters staff was required, and I was it. It was my mistake for not leaving as soon as I got up. The others get up on Sundays, throw a uniform over pajamas, and catch a cyclo downtown. For a small consideration, the madames allow them to sleep in used cubicles until early afternoon. They must get out when the girls begin to bring in clients. By that time it is safe to go about the day's business.

I reported and was sent to the general's office. A congressman was coming through to see the corps. An update was needed for the display map. The sergeant major would give me the needed instructions. I would draw cardboard and coloring equipment from the supply sergeant.

I thought of a German construction worker I had met on a summer job. At coffee break, as he dozed on the table, he would raise his head from time to time for stories about the war. The other men listened to him, not because they had not been there themselves, not because they necessarily believed him (his stories were often out of chronology), but because he told it so it *sounded* real. He had known Rommel and had a picture to prove it. On the back, it read "To my friend Al Schubert"; at least that is what Al translated. In the picture Al had all his teeth.

Previous Al had marched on Paris. On a cold night he and his comrades had stood in line for three hours only to have the madame appear and turn them away. He had just reached the door. The line was still a block long. But we are Germans! We have won, he shouted. Walking like a snake, she closed the door. Perhaps it was in France, maybe Poland or Belgium, that he was shot in the intestines. A near miss, he showed the scar at shower time. Of course I will live, but how about der thing? The doctor had applied rooster skin, and der thing was able to boast of postwar children. How could he have been in all those places? The men forgot that for his country the war lasted six years. They had taken on the world, after all. A young German in those days . . .

On the way to Stalingrad everyone died. His best friend and the officers. Since he put the body only three feet under, he made a map and hoped to return for a more proper burial. He became platoon leader. The platoon was under strength, so they sent him one boy with a sniper rifle. Every time the boy fired, he had to take out a notebook and write it down. He loaded one bullet at a time. Once he got two Russians with a single shot; Al slapped both knees. Al tried to teach him to keep down, but they got him at Stalingrad.

At Stalingrad, everyone died. Al was convinced that he had been made a captain, but the people who promoted him died. The headquarters was captured, and he never got the pay. On the retreat he reburied the friend, whose hair had grown shoulder length and was tangled in the earth like young roots. The Russians captured him, he had no shoes, and he was shipped to Siberia. It was in Siberia that the rest of his teeth fell

113

out. That summer, as we built the roof of a factory, Al gummed food. He was between sets of teeth, being able now to purchase a more expensive pair. The German union card had stood him in good stead as a mason.

In Siberia everybody died again. Not only was he not promoted, he was given up for dead. Outside Stalingrad, said the letter. His family did not even receive his army pay, although it eventually got a small death stipend. It worked for the good, though, because his wife was too busy working to remarry. When he was repatriated after six years in Siberia, they left for America as fast as they could. The hell with people who follow dictators and lost wars! He had his citizen papers now.

Warsaw, Paris, Tobruk, El Alamein, Stalingrad, Siberia . . .

Duc Hoa, Tuy Hoa, My Tho, Dong Tam, Cai Be, Nam Can, Cai Cai, Bac Lieu . . .

Can Tho. I cut out triangular pennants for unit decals. There were rectangles for flags, and crayons. The sergeant major had a supply of tiny eagles. He showed me how to do the towns. Duc Hoa . . .

Bac Lieu, a pennant indicating divisional head-quarters. Sa Dec the same. Border camps Cai Cai and Cai Be. Khaki pennants to signify irregular forces. I added the border camps and colored in spaces under friendly and enemy control. Then marginal areas.

The general patted my shoulder and said I had done a good job. They couldn't make it around here without me. For once, everything was perfect. Spelled right. Towns at proper coordinates. The scale was perfect, and the visual effect appropriate. Since my day was shot anyway, the general wanted me to stick around and hold the A-frame. I could also pull charts.

The congressman arrived wearing fatigues without insignia. I wondered if he would take them home; his name was taped in black lettering above the right pocket. I am sure the depot offers each congressman the uniform he uses—to keep as a gift. Some probably take them to show friends. Others remove the name and return the suit for use by an actual soldier. These can brag to their friends of incorruptibility in small matters.

Like many men who are fat on television, the congressman was thinner in person. His face seemed almost ruddy instead of pockmarked. The congressman and the general shook hands. The general introduced me as the soldier who escorted the Christmas comedian.

The general pointed to an overnight bag, which I carried to the jeep. The congressman smiled. He was clearly impressed at being met by generals and having his bags carried by men who carried bags for celebrities. He was attentive to each part of the surroundings: the metal grating (of which the airfield was composed), the helicopters, even the steel bars holding up the canvas canopy of the jeep. He ran his hand across the canvas like a tourist buying on the Persian market. It reminded me of small-town visitors in a New York hotel, thinking the furniture a sort of cultural display. The woodwork and rugs, too. They wonder what it costs and whether the company would ship like material to their town. They ring bells to see if attendants will come. The actual bellboy, because he has a face, and consequently imperfections, is not at all what they would have suspected. But even though he is not the butler on television, they are impressed. The general, remembering that I do not drive, said that he enjoyed driving and got into the driver's seat himself. Highest-paid chauffeur you'll ever have, he said to me. This manner made quite a hit with the congressman.

"So this is the Mekong Delta. It all started here."

"Yes," said the general. "That's what they say in the briefings."

"Well, I guess that makes this some sort of historic spot."

Over the headquarters gate are the Roman numeral four and some words in Vietnamese. The congressman asked if Kublai Khan had built the area. The general said he understood it had been the French. Must be hell to have everything in your country built by somebody else, said the congressman.

The officers were waiting in the briefing room. Rachow was absent, but I heard the general say that tomorrow Rachow would be flying the visitor around. The congressman was introduced by the general as a distinguished public servant who had had a big hand in military appropriations, who is a friend of the fighting man, who understands the necessity . . .

Each officer had his own overlay for the map. The general gave the overall briefing. I stood behind the A-frame, and when he tapped it with his swagger stick, I pulled aside another chart. As he came to my map, the general began describing a hard-fought game of Monopoly. They held Pennsylvania Avenue. We've got Park Place. They have the Reading and one other railroad, it slips his mind but is not important. We have Baltic Avenue with a hotel on it. St. James Place is partially developed: we're clearing out the VC and have already built two houses on it! The red stars, you see, are Charlie, and the flags and eagles us.

As he spoke, I conceived the peculiar notion that before a satisfactory war could be fought, men such as this must be killed off or pushed aside. The congressman asked if we lacked for anything, and the general said that, of course, we could always use more of everything, but that basically the situation was in hand. The congressman nodded, proud of his newly

116

gained expertise. He jotted down technical lingo in a notebook. He could spring it on his constituents in the hill country. A press release, perhaps, or a newsletter from their man on the scene. For a month his correspondence could begin, "I just got back from Vietnam and found your letter waiting on my desk . . ."

As the voices rattled on, I inspected the map for which I had given up my Sunday. I had held the contrast to a minimum, so that there was no black or white on it. Only different weavings of gray shading, ourselves and the enemy, and flags and eagles, and broken lines.

★ nineteen ★

RACHOW WAS IN AND OUT in the morning, staying only long enough to leave some memos. Mooney frowned.

"That man has been in the army long enough to know what the chain of command is."

I begged pardon.

"Putting work directly on your desk. He goes to you through me, and I'm going to talk to him about it."

Numerous, uncounted rotations of the fan.

"I should have known a pilot wouldn't be up on administration."

He paused.

"You and me got to run the whole office. You know where he is during the day? I found out from the sergeant major over the weekend. He flies a helicopter out to the operations areas. That's where he is. He comes here at night."

I got up and picked the outgoing memos out of Mooney's box. I made an unnecessary trip to the message center. On the way I met the message runner. He was collecting memos. Ignoring him, I delivered them myself. I stopped at the bathroom, which was part of the message center building. I had only a dribble. Just the same I took my time. No matter how you shake and dance . . . The last few drops . . . Will

. . . Your pants . . . Someone had beeen writing on the wall, a daily revision of his days remaining. He began with two hundred and sixty-one and had crossed off each succeeding day down to fifty-two. I made a note to bring pencil and write a message of some sort before he left. I returned to the office and took out a memo to type. The fan turned slowly.

"And when he's not doing that, he's hanging around the TOC all night. Listening to radio reports. You'd think he was looking for trouble."

"Who's that?"

"The colonel, ass. Don't you ever listen from the beginning?"

Mooney was sorting paperwork. Most of his job seemed to involve judgmental matters with piles of papers. He held a paper in each hand, and his eyes shifted from left to right as though the papers were alternative pieces for a puzzle.

More or less as an afterthought on the conversation, he leaned forward and said confidentially, "He sure as hell has a fucked-up concept of administration."

At noon there was a letter from E. She, too, is beginning to find the war in conflict with her feelings. "Pacifist sensitivity," she calls it. For a moment, I thought she had tired of her form letter. But no, she respects, even in error, my "commitment." It is apparent that I will have to bone up on vocabulary before going home: I had not thought the word "commitment" to have connotation of absolute moral value. Beneath a cynical veneer, she goes on, I am an old-fashioned patriot, dedicated to the propagation of parliamentary democracy. My error is pardonable.

I liked that especially. She hates war, but finds the warrior charming. In the next issue of her letter, however, I will point out that there is a difference between "pacifism" and chivalry. We are a nation of

119

imprecise speakers, and perhaps the distinction has escaped her. To be perfectly fair, the two may have very nearly the same meaning under ordinary suburban circumstance.

She concludes, "You are the kind of spirit who is morally untouched by the wrongs he may commit." There, I must admit, she has put her finger on it. Just as I see myself a virginity perpetually renewed by a night's sleep and virtuous dreams. Or rather, as I sometimes choose to believe, an actor whose inhumanities are necessary to the plot. Whose victims are straw people. The point of a drama is not its carnage but how the hero turns out.

If Hamlet should learn calculus: "To be or not to be," he would say, and stop abruptly. He would note that one's lifetime is a finite payload of relative certainty, while death or life after (be there ever so slight a chance of it) is beyond the measurable. Pascal's wager: Even in matters of life and death one's course of action may be determined by mathematics. "Very well," Hamlet would say, "but I am not Pascal. How shall I say it? We have different . . . preference curves." *To be or not to be*, again. He stops, again. The difference between Hamlet and Pascal is a matter of data, so Hamlet would collect a data base, establish affinities, collect more data, and feed it into a computer, and find that result . . .

★ twenty ★

THE LONGER ONE is in the army, the harder it is to distinguish what has happened from the war stories he has heard. Certain stories make the rounds of training camps. Some happen with universality; others no longer do. The stories are told by instructors. Little effort is made to distinguish between first-person and third-person telling. In the next telling, the same becomes the case with the troops. An atmosphere develops in which everything a person hears is taken into his backlog of private experience.

Certain things are universal. There is a boy from the mountains in every barracks; he sits on his bunk at night and on weekends writing letters to his family and reading from the Bible. He has probably not read so much of the Bible in his entire life, but recalls the warning of a local minister that in the stress of far places and evil companions, he will wish to turn to it. There is a young man who has no reason for being there but anomaly itself; he is at pains to explain his wealth, breeding, and the luxuries to which he is accustomed, and of which he is being deprived. I was almost, but not quite, that man. Instead, there was a sociology major who dropped out of school his sophomore year. As often as not, this man is over six feet three and has personal problems. At least one of the above persons is a near statistical certainty in every barracks.

There are several categories of event. There is the surprise inspection. It follows a command lecture on the sanctity of a personal firearm, the inspection timed for everyone to have just forgotten the warning. The sociology major, with his rusty weapon gigged, is standing next to the one recruit who happens to have cleaned his weapon, for no reason, the night before. "You're a goddamned anal retentive," the sociologist says in a stage whisper. On the other side of the barracks one of the men slips and calls his rifle a "gun," one of the great taboos, like calling a ship a boat or a sergeant sir. Every recruit knows, is laboriously shown on the very first day, that the barrel has rifling in it. imparting spin to the projectile, and thus there and forever removing from itself the nomenclature "gun." The recruit, as the story goes, is the shy one with feelings of inadequacy; he is ordered to walk around for a week with rifle on shoulder and fly open, other weapon in other hand, incanting,

> This is my rifle, and
> This is my gun.
> One is for shooting,
> The other for fun.

Inspections of this sort have taken place because of the arrival of a new commander, in midstream, shaky in the performance of his functions, unable to find real duties, and determined to find *something* to do. The other inspection occurs at three A.M., the men being awakened by a kick on the foot of their bunks. It is the battalion doctor along with the company commander and a member of company cadre. The sociologist whispers that the commander and medical personnel are a group of "goddamn sado-masochists."

One of the men, who was in the navy before, got out, and rejoined in the army, says that it's "a short-arm inspection." No one understands this except for one career soldier's son and one recruit who reads adventure magazines. The men are lined up in their underwear and made, one by one, to drop their pants, the doctor saying, "All right, milk it down." It is reminiscent of grade-school spankings. The ones with drip have names written down and are told to report after reveille. The men vaguely remember the cadre sergeant saying, as he turned on the lights, "All right, troopers, pecker check. Nobody goes to the latrine." The one who said "gun" and the one with the perfect rifle are trembling, although they are pronounced "clean." The one whose father was in the army is whistling a tune, to which the words . . . an old song . . . Does it hang low? does it wobble to and fro? can you tie it in a knot? can you tie it in a bow? can you throw it over your shoulder, like a continental soldier?

The need for data is obvious.

★ twenty-one ★

Rachow has an assistant. A novelist would make much of the fact that he is Negro. I'm not sure how to go about it. It's too difficult. I don't know enough about him. Only that he drinks every night at the aviation club. White soldiers do that too. Maybe the liquor tastes different when one is black. They call him K.C. He's from Kansas City.

He's nice enough to me. Perhaps he holds things back. If so, it is probably that he is Rachow's crew chief and I am only a clerical aide. He tells me the story of his life over drinks. It never comes out the same. Maybe that's his way of warning me that he's not on the level. Just the same, a lot of it has to be true. He is probably just a great embellisher.

I think Rachow *sent* him to have a drink with me. The old man must want to see how I really feel about things. What it does prove is that the old man trusts him. I guess I should take his stories more literally. He has lined it up for me to go on some kind of mission. Rachow probably sensed that I was restless.

He is persistent. Having a drink with me was not an easy thing. I ordered orange soda. Another one came each time he ordered a beer. He wanted to know what was wrong that I didn't drink. I told him it was habit. I had formed the habit when I had venereal

124

disease. Drinking inflames the urinary tract. The doctor made me lay off. It was the simple truth. As soon as I said it to K.C., I realized that I went on abstaining just as I went on doing calisthenics. It compensates for the lack of hardship. Otherwise I would feel guilty, pampered. It is a penance.

K.C. tells his life story over and over again. It's the only thing he knows. It's different every time, as if he were God, and all he had to do all day were to make up new histories for K.C. He avoids the details of his birth and sticks to the moments of insight and decisive action. He usually begins his story near the end of it, after he became a helicopter gunner.

At one point he was removed from flying duty and was put on special assignment at an air force headquarters. The sergeant major led him into a storeroom full of cardboard boxes. Each one contained twenty-four model airplane kits. The glue was enclosed. He was given an hour to read and master the directions. Then he began assembling them. The sergeant major, not entirely satisfied with his progress, imposed a production quota. As soon as they were done they were hauled away and put in glass display cases. In front of them was a written description of characteristics copied from relevant directives. Some were mounted for desk-tops. Others were wired and suspended from the ceiling. The ones left over were to be assembled also and sent to orphanages for war waifs. K.C. walked in on a full colonel having a dogfight in the middle of his office with two of the planes suspended from the ceiling. The sound of their motors, as rendered, was the same as my uncle's Lancasters; no technological advance there. The colonel, in a fit of enthusiasm, had even smashed a wing with his fist. When they caught K.C. throwing rocks at the glass case in front of headquarters, it was the same colonel that demanded he be sent to the stockade . . .

A stockade guard he met at the beer hall had told him of a certain practice. The guard stood in the tower with his carbine trained on the prisoners, now one, now another. Slowly he let the slack out of the trigger, seeing how close it could come to release without releasing a round. They aimed at the backs of heads and the testicles. It was a product of boredom, the grossly unfair four-hour shifts. K.C. had been out of the stockade only a week.

A few days later the platoon sergeant had taken him behind the barracks for a licking. K.C. had eight gigs on command inspection, and quoted the sergeant: wasn't any funky black-ass nigger going to keep him from making E-7. But K.C. managed to kick him "up between the running lights," and get his licks in. They called him to the orderly room and told him that he was going back to the stockade. It was only a matter of the time required for paperwork.

K.C. managed to get a gun and bury it in a lock-box off the compound. He waited to be formally charged. First he would go to the orderly room. The first shot would be the field first, who was big and might require a second. Then the first sergeant and company clerk. Then the commander, who would be bottled up in his office and couldn't escape. As he planned the attack, for the first time in his life, he felt like a real soldier. He would circle back to the mess hall and shoot the first cook, but spare the mess sergeant, who had done him no wrong.

Just planning it had made him a better soldier. If he was going to do all that, he was going to have his house in order when he did it.

He would hold up the ordnance room for ammunition. He would change to an automatic weapon. That would be the first real danger point; if they were alert, they would get him there. If not, on to the next headquarters! He had made a map, and had re-

126

hearsed the path over and over. He devised contigency plans in case he encountered resistance. There were also alternative targets. At the next headquarters was a detail sergeant who had been grossly unfair and of course the commandant. He made a sketch of the building.

They were almost certain to get him there. He had a favorite spot picked out to hole up and shoot it out to the death.

As he told of his plan, it became so real to him that he spoke of it as actually happening. His tone took me completely off guard.

"Good God, man," I said, "it's a good thing we're fighting on the same side!" Once having said it, I had to decide what I meant.

Colonel Rachow had been appointed to investigate the incident of the platoon sergeant. K.C. had been cleared, and further investigation went so far as to decry his earlier punishments and have them stricken from the record. Shortly afterward he became Rachow's crew chief, and has held the position ever since.

K.C. speaks of Rachow as if the colonel were an extension of himself. Rachow does things and K.C. appreciates them. One is Quixote, the other Panza. I am almost afraid to go flying with them. It will make me feel like Cervantes grabbing a donkey and sallying forth after the two of them. Taking notes. I wouldn't want K.C. to stop telling stories merely because I was there. The pleasure is in the telling anyway.

It was from K.C. that I learned of the dénouement with the congressman. The general had brought the congressman to the airfield in order to show him an operations area. He had made the congressman put on a flak jacket on the ground. The man was sweating before he got in the chopper. He smelled like burnt starch.

Then Rachow pulled back the stick and shut his eyes. He could do it, K.C. said. The copilot didn't believe it. He believed he squinted very small and sneaked, but K.C. knew he did it, and wouldn't mind flying with him even if he had a blindfold. Rachow had been around more than a year longer than K.C. had been around. The copilot, who used to be exec when Rachow was battalion commander, had not been around at all. The last exec had left early with a physical problem, of which K.C. had his suspicions. The gunners were changed every month or two. They got nervous breakdowns.

Rachow, however, had flown the same spots so often that he only had to look which way he had parked the chopper. He could take off and fly ninety miles with his eyes shut. Only the landing required vision, and if he had dozed off, K.C. remembered to wake him. Some men got on it and didn't know which way to turn, Rachow got on it, you could bet he could navigate by freckles to say nothing of ordinary woman's features. He could draw a map of the corps on his wife's. . .

The congressman, whom K.C. referred to as "the vip," sweating before he was scared, began reaching around for straps to batten down with. The copilot sat back with his arms folded, as instructed. Rachow didn't like interference when he was flying. When the congressman tried to strike up a conversation, Rachow insisted that silence be maintained over the intercom for all but tactical matters. He set the congressman to looking for antiaircraft guns.

Halfway to the operations area, Rachow snapped awake and called back on the intercom to K.C., asking if there was some sort of identifiable landmark below. K.C. started to say but Rachow interrupted him.

He asked the congressman if he saw any antiaircraft. Rachow was quiet, then mumbled some complaints about wind velocity, control calibration, and the necessity to avoid flak zones. The congressman wanted to ask questions, but Rachow cut him off with technical talk. Next Rachow asked K.C. pointblank if he thought they might have strayed into Cambodia. That was the point where the congressman leaned forward with his head between his knees and threw up. Why in hell, Rachow wanted to know, had we given those jets to the Cambodian air force?

In a few minutes they were above the stagefield. The copilot had his hands folded across his chest. He wanted hands off the whole mess. Rachow could get everybody killed or court-martialed if he wanted to; that's what K.C. supposed he was thinking. Nobody ever thought Rachow was going to get away with anything, but K.C. had been around for two years and Rachow had gotten away with everything. He would rather get away with things than be a general, said K.C. The copilot is careful not to touch Rachow in case it might be catching.

Rachow asked the congressman if he had seen the flak bursts out the left door, and the congressman said he had. There had been no flak bursts. Rachow offered him a carbine to hold while going home in case they went low enough to do any firing. The congressman said that the flight had been the finest military experience of his life, and he was a veteran of two wars, although in each case he had not really been at the front, and that Rachow was the finest example of military bearing and dedication he had seen, and a credit to the air force. Rachow explained politely that he was a member of the army. The congressman recognized the insignia at once. When the congressman had been introduced around the stagefield tent, and set down at a table with a Vietnamese general, an interpreter, doughnuts, and milk, Rachow said to K.C.,

"There sits a man who is going to go home and tell his wife a mother of a story."

It is a firm commitment now—I am to go on a mission. This coming weekend Rachow will give me a lift to the stagefield.

A few days ago he brought up the fact that he knew of a Ranger unit short of advisers. He couldn't spare me, of course, on a permanent basis. I would go on being his assistant. However, there was no reason for me not to go out with the Rangers every now and then. The adviser, after all, was nothing more than a presence. It was purely bearing, the authentic Roman shoring up the mercenaries. Quite often his own sorties coincided with a Ranger operation. In light of this fact, he could even give me a lift to the stagefield. He had already spoken to Mooney. As a formality, I must do Mooney the courtesy of a request. Mooney, he reminded me, had a noncom's touchiness about authority. Just say: Mooney, I hope you will have no objection to my seeing a litte action on my day off.

In the meantime, I have already made a leaflet flight with Rachow and K.C. It was at night, and we circled the mouth of the Mekong dumping out crates of paper.

The groundfire came up in flashes like unsuspected sparks from a dead fire. The machine gun bursts came up in long chains of red and orange golf balls. The fifty calibers were baseball size. They headed for the ship, then veered to the side, missing us fifty yards when they appeared ten feet away. If one of the golf balls stayed very still, growing larger and larger, it hit part of the ship with a metallic sound. We stood in the open doors and shouted challenges a thousand feet down.

"Come on you bastards, mix it up. I paid good

130

money for this goddamn seat. Let's see some punches. Candy asses!"

"Come on, nick me so I can get a Purple Heart."

Our machine guns useless in the dark, we poured a barrage of mucus and urine upon the countryside.

As K.C. unbuttoned his fly, I recalled my childhood wish to see the heavens open and an airliner empty its toilets on the head of the corner cop.

"You mothers that can't swim better head for the sampans."

I had been probing to find out the source of K.C.'s loyalty. He has extended twice in Vietnam with an order on his papers that he be allowed to stay on as Rachow's crew chief. Has the old man offered him an island?

The best I can get out of him is something he whispered in the bar. He has the most vivid picture of his own funeral. White dignitaries, friends, and family, the genteel blacks of Kansas City all filing by for a last look at his dick-down corpse. He is staying in Vietnam conditionally. Rachow has sworn, he says, that if he receives a mortal wound, the body will be flown to a piece of impenetrable terrain—the mangroves, or the Plain of Reeds, or the U Minh Forest—and there will be dropped into a swamp.

★ twenty-two ★

SATURDAY MORNING K.C. came to fetch me. I woke the supply sergeant to draw a carbine and was given a death curse. If I wanted to die at four A.M. I should have the courtesy to draw equipment the day before.

The drive to the airfield split the town down the middle. There slept thirty, perhaps ninety thousand people. One cannot be sure. It is the nature of such a town to defy the census. It presents an optical illusion like the picture with silhouettes of two ladies. Let your vision blur and the hag's nose becomes the bodice of a young girl. In this town a single residence may divide in three. How cozy it seemed before dawn! It was as if an architect had chosen to build a masterpiece of packing crates.

At the edge of town we passed a bridge and could see the sun. It had bounced fully dressed from its bed beneath the horizon. Standing in the eastern sky, it had the effect of an orange candle, dripping wax. The old charioteer wanted to serve notice that he, at least, had not changed in his bearing since the windy plains of Troy.

On the road we met two carts going to market. One contained a snake in a cage. Torpid already from the sun, he lay in loops as two boys poked at him with sticks. Apparently they were marking off the choice

132

cuts of meat. The second cart contained a dead hog, strapped to the floor with his head hanging off the edge. A white slime still dripped from his nostrils. When a third vehicle approached, K.C. warned me to hold my nose. He mumbled something about the meat wagon. It was the military hearse. Stacked on slabs like a multidecker sandwich were the residue of local battlefields. Some were yesterday's, others a week old, but only now recoverable.

Have I begun inventing things? A man who goes to a war should return with tales to tell. God knows, I would like to take part in tellable stories. Is my life merging with my imagination? I must examine the plausibility of each step I take now that something is about to happen. If only M. were here to critique my day's activities, I could be sure. Even E. I remember that once, after I changed the part of my hair, I made a calculation daily for several months. I wanted to know what proportion of my life had been spent with the new part; in other words, whether time and custom had lent my appearance plausibility.

A dream pursues me. In it my role is more or less heroic. That is to say that I am on the right side of some sort of event and am committing some sort of act. The preliminary plot of the dream is always forgotten, perhaps repressed, but in the end I am shooting at a large number of men. I am alone. I am a desperate shooter, racing madly after them. I fire my weapon, but they refuse to fall. This vexes me, but I do not stop firing, completely in desperation. They refuse to fall, but so, for some reason, do I, although they are armed.

That such a situation can exist in my dreams is disturbing. The dream recurs, and leaves off with me still frantically shooting; perhaps the bullets have not had time yet to find their marks. From one point of view, that of a certain philosopher, I suppose that the dream is easily explainable. My targets and I are at different levels of reality. I am quite real. I shoot from a position entrenched in reality, but they are shadows. They are no more than the stage props in *Hamlet*. If they should fall, I should by rights be startled. Of course, it would only be acting. Sir Isaac: people are real in proportion with their density, and inversely with their distance squared. Men who fire pistols are murderers; men who fire howitzers, actors. Men who shoot wives and mothers? Einsteins, perhaps. Madmen who trample Newton's Law.

On the side of the helicopter there is an inscription. K.C. asked if they might put one where most ships have something like "The Wobbly Duck" or "One-Eyed Jack" or "Big Dick from Boston." He asked Rachow to suggest a fitting inscription. The two lines read,

> Those that I fight I do not hate
> Those that I guard I do not love

At first K.C. found the lines strange. Rachow got them out of a book. The more K.C. had time to think, the better he liked them. He decided that they had an occult meaning, for him alone: poetry is that way. Certainly no one else has such an inscription. It gives the ship a kind of class. The copilot thought Rachow would never get away with it, but he does, and the inscription is not covered over even for VIPs.

Rachow introduced me to the Ranger advisers. The captain was a tall man with light coloring, and his sergeant was almost as tall. The sergeant was fat with the sort of weight which betrays the neatest military clothes. Heavy starch in his fatigue jacket could not contain his belly overhang. Just above the buckle was a large indentation for a fat man's navel. The captain was under thirty and the sergeant near forty. Both men had short hair. Their looks struck me as harbingers of superficiality. Not stupidity, not explicabilty; everyone may at some level be reduced to these. Everything appeared on the surfaces. The captain's crew cut looked carefully washed and then waxed to stand straight up. I could see the skin of his scalp through the bristles, and it too seemed coated with wax. It was as if long hair might conceal secrets, real or spurious. In its depths there might be little wads of chewing gum or mucus or seminal fluid.

It was arranged that I would go with the point squad of a certain company. It had apparently not occurred to the Rangers that I might be untrustworthy. They trusted me implicitly for standing before them as a volunteer with a carbine. There would be no supervision, none from them to me, and little from me to the native Rangers. They gave me a map with a destination circled. It was a small village, a suspected sanctuary. I was to see that the Rangers got there, that they did not stop to plunder prematurely or get sidetracked. In all likelihood we would meet no opposition. Once there they were on their own. It was agreed that Rachow would pick me up at the village as he returned from the day's operations.

It was like a long morning hike, the scenery much more varied than I had imagined it. Flights of jets seemed to punctuate the half hours. From time to time we stopped and watched them as they peeled out of formation one by one and made their parabolas at suspected enemy targets. All the positions were well ahead of us, but we could see the black smoke from napalm, and occasionally the rich orange fire. There was less noise than I had suspected, but we may have been further back than I realized.

The Rangers were uncomfortable in my presence. It was clear that they preferred having no adviser at all.

They seemed to think that my presence might be inhibiting in some way. There was an interpreter, in uniform without rank. I had to make him repeat each phrase he spoke. He told me that he was much better at written English and should have been kept in a headquarters job. The sergeant plunged ahead of me, making it doubly clear that my services would not be required. He too was fat and approaching middle age. There is, I thought, a bit of universality to the non-commissioned officer. Although his uniform was starched to be crisper than those of his men, he too overhung his belt, with evidence of a fat man's navel on the underroll.

After several hours we emerged on a plain of clearer terrain. For miles ahead there were more or less level paddies without obstructions to vision. This was either a good omen or an assurance of actual safety, for the men began talking, smiling, and slapping backs. They were apparently having a laugh on me, as they came together in groups of two or three to giggle and turn in my direction. One of them smiled and held up his fist; it was impossible to tell if his mood was hostility or comradeship. Perhaps he himself was unsure. "Tonight," he shouted, "tonight," and burst into a giggle when I cocked my head to indicate that I couldn't get his meaning. Another said something to the interpreter. The interpreter dutifully translated; the men wanted me to know that tonight after I left they would have a fine time with the Viet Cong women. At first subduing them, he said, and then by subtle degrees enjoying them. Americans could not understand such subtlety. Whether by anger, cruelty, honesty, or curiosity I do not know, but I snapped back to the interpreter that he must tell them the anecdote by which we were cautioned in Saigon; that we must be sure to bring our own condoms because theirs were inadequate in size. Again he dutifully translated, and they were silent. It was about a half hour before they began to resume the banter. At that time another flight of strafing jets created a break in the chain of thought and a topic for renewed comment.

We resumed the march, and within a few hundred meters were in sight of the village. Even at a great distance it was possible to detect first signs of the damage inflicted by the jets. The whole side of town nearest us had been burned out by napalm. It was still smoking, even burning in spots, and charred remainders of huts stood up like skeletons. I took out my map to be sure that it was the correct village. Strange, I thought, that I could not recall it from the map I made for the general, but the war in the field and the war in the offices were two very different things. Population was deceptive to begin with in such nations as this, and with the roving herds of refugees it may have recently swelled to the size on the Ranger map, or it might be just under the size required for depletion on the general's. At any rate, there was little question that it was the objective.

The near side of town, I saw, was definitely burned to the skeleton. The center was only strafed. The enemy had pulled out. As I got closer I saw that this was not entirely true; some had pulled out in time, but by no means all. With a fair mixture of the native population the enemy was plastered from one end of town to the other. At the sight of the first corpse, the Rangers let out a whoop and began talking and laughing as loudly as before. The sergeant spun around with his automatic rifle and fired into a clump of bushes. He wiped the back of his hand across his mouth as if he had been eating with his fingers. The other men began to catch on, firing into the air, into houses, and trees, into corpses. The men behind us stopped. It was necessary to radio back not to worry, that resistance was minimal.

Implausibility is my enemy. My life must remain believable, I kept thinking. I asked at each pause: Will M. buy this? Will E.? Would a person if he read about it? I feared that I was tramping, step by step, in the direction of the implausible. Was it possible that my life was becoming like that of a literary device? An actor in a novel, or perhaps a memoir? What if I went down in the end? How would I be handled? Would I become what is called a "tragedy"? I decided that if I die, and am around to see it, it will rank as tragedy. Otherwise only a corpse.

There was even a body on one of the roofs. How he happened to be there and be killed by strafing aircraft I will never imagine. Others were leaned against the walls in the alleys, occasionally with evidence that some effort had been made to put them in order before the hasty retreat. The corpses did not bother me. I felt only the mild injunction to tread lightly that comes to a small boy who steps on a dead bird and collects feathers on his shoes.

The squad turned aside at the center of town. There was a little adjunct a half mile off to the side. It appeared on no maps at all. We in the point squad were to wait there alone. There Rachow was to pick me up. The men were now quite happy. We passed attractive and half-clad girls. Daughters and wives of routed enemy. The Rangers were transformed—smiles, ribaldry, laughter from the lewdest depths. "Tonight, tonight," they began to shout again, for my benefit. They were weaving in and out of formation to slap each other on the back. Each man in turn came over to slap my back. One held his rifle between his legs, slanting upward at an acute angle. He stroked the barrel slowly up and down. Soon they were all holding their rifles between their legs.

The adjunct looked the same as the town, only without so much burning. Strafing had done the job. I saw another corpse on a roof. The Rangers turned up an alley. The way there was literally strewn with corpses. It had been either an assembly point for casualties or a headquarters from which men had poured out to be strafed.

The Rangers appeared not at all disappointed that air power had won their battle. They continued firing their weapons at all angles. "Tonight, tonight." The leader of the frolicking began masturbating the barrel again and fired from between his legs. At the end of the alley were cages of chickens and ducks. The men shouted "tonight" to a pair of waifs, who could be seen in a doorway hiding behind their mother. The sergeant issued a command, and the men rushed to the cages of fowl. They knocked in the cages with rifle butts, freeing a few of the birds and grabbing the others to wring their necks. Then they made a division of labor. Two unsheathed their bayonets for spits. Others began cleaning birds. The old woman rushed at the sergeant and was thrown to the ground. The Rangers began throwing carcasses into a pile, the heads carefully pointed the same way. One soldier, a short man with fat lips, had taken out his cleaning rod, for the rifle bore. He began using it, literally, to commit rape upon one of the she-ducks. He held the duck under his arm, trapping its legs in the webbing of his gear. He was pithing it from the posterior end, impaling it deeper and deeper on the cleaning rod. It was honking with increasing desperation, perhaps so blinded with pain and death that its involuntary nervous system had taken over the response.

The Rangers were together in a cluster. I counted to be certain. Noting my distance, I kneeled as if to tie a shoe. I made a check of my carbine, released the safety, and tugged on my extra clips. They protruded from the belt pouches in correct position for rapid reload. Then I turned the cycle selector to automatic fire. I remembered the admonition to squeeze slowly rather than jerking.

It never ceases to seem incongruous that real guns make only a vague clack rather the bang and echo represented in movies. The man pithing the duck and the two with spits fell backward. They resembled marionettes jerked from behind. My dream, I thought, has caught up with me. Rather I did not think so then, but later. Then I was noticing that my carbine was overoiled; a splash of oil hit me in the right cheek. I could smell it and feel it dripping toward my mouth. I could taste the metallic tang of food from a rusty can. All the men were down but their sergeant; he was running in a crouch inside the hut. The old lady was with him. He was fumbling with his rifle. I unhooked a grenade from my belt, and remembering the release estimate from basic, plus the standard deviation—I forget what that is called in training—I held the grenade for two seconds and threw it into the hut. Unlike the movies, again, grenades are never to be lobbed—a myth held over from the old concussion type, I suppose—but are spiraled when possible, and always thrown with a football motion. I waited an instant without counting. The sergeant came flying through the wall. The old lady as well.

After the noise, this time with an echo, I expected silence. I heard instead the sound of helicopter rotors. Above me, not thirty yards away, was Rachow's ship. I snapped back to a waking state. Around me were only corpses, in dramatic disarray. I would be tried and made an example of. Others would exorcise their bad consciences at my expense. I began to think of the dream. No story could save me, because it would be my word against that of a full colonel.

I boarded the ship. Nothing was said.

☆ *part three* ☆

★ twenty-three ★

THIS MORNING I woke before dawn and stepped outside to wait for the sunrise. Perhaps there was a bit of excitement for the day's events, although yesterday I had felt sure that I would be quite blasé. Walking to the guard turret, where I could look out on the countryside, I was reminded that toothaches have an affinity for the period just before the sun. It is the cooler air, which gets into the hollows of the grinders. The feeling is the same as that from a coating of lemon tartar. Coffee tartar the same. A teeth on edge sort of thing. It will come off with a good brushing. One must be careful, then, just the same, as the teeth have a surprisingly good memory for shock to their fibers.

It gave a slightly odd sensation to watch the first pastel appear on the east horizon. This was followed by a general lighting up, as if a lamp were being brought around a corner. In childhood I had thought of the great wars as a time when the skies were continuously dark for four years. I even related my notion to a passage from Homer, in which projectiles hide the sun. Or perhaps that association was an afterthought. Still, this war in no way suits my myth: a banker's sun was on the way. With the light fully committed, I went inside for a cold shower. I was still well in ad-

vance of my comrades. How M. mocked my showers!
And the notion that bouncing out of bed is a determinant of character!

The battalions in green fatigues and red tunics march into the courtyard. The American-made helmets, I note each time I see them, give them the appearance of midgets. Their short legs shuffled along, bending too loosely at the knees for a genuine march, as though they were aware of participation in a parody. The brass band appeared from behind a building: I had heard them tuning up. A brass band, like a battle, must be whole hog, I thought; a halfway effort won't do. The generals appeared at the front of the headquarters, each carrying his swagger stick. The Vietnamese general is new. They walked to the reviewing stand almost side by side without exchanging a word or a glance. The American looked at his wristwatch; he was ahead of schedule. Messengers were hurrying from office to office, hoping to beat the music. Others were hiding indoors, waiting for it to end before they came out. A full colonel broke into a trot in the direction of the message center. Suddenly the first note sounded, the national anthems. The colonel dropped the papers to his side, transferred them quickly to his left hand, and braced to salute with his right. The scene froze; time stood still; everywhere around the courtyard travelers caught in motion reverted to a brace and saluted the flag. Then the music stopped and motion resumed as if the reel had been spliced and let go to run again. Only the little fellows remained at attention. Then, watching them glance from inside the oversize helmets, a strange thought hit me: we are at war with midgets! I recalled a line from Woodrow Wilson, that there is such a thing as having too much pride to go to war with an enemy who is hopelessly outclassed.

146

The photographer came out of the freeze and pointed his camera so as to catch the general, myself, and the medal. I could see it in the general's hand. The Cross of Gallantry had jagged edges unlike the Honor Medal, which had smooth. The general leaned forward at my lapel and the photographer fired twice. Then, as I have seen him do dozens of times before, the general handed the certificate from his left hand to the left of the recipient, myself, while our rights crossed over to shake. The full medal hung on my lapel for the last time. After the ceremony one wears only the ribbon. The ribbon has the colors of the cloth part, but is only a symbol of the medal itself. The few times I have seen actual medals, they have been worn by civilians, not an uncommon sight on lapels in news photos from France or Russia.

Why, I asked myself, had Rachow chosen to report what he did? It is possible that he made an honest error. He arrived, apparently, at the conclusion of a ferocious battle. The adjunct of the town alone had not been evacuated; rather the Cong had laid a last ambush, a squad of sappers, to rob the Rangers of their victory. Caught in a crossfire, hundreds of yards apart from the main force, their ammunition used up in high jinks, worse yet, unaware of their surroundings because of their preoccupation with the slaughter of a cache of fowl . . . Evidence of the battle, the situation, was literally plastered across the scene. The enemy had even fired from rooftops. One had died there. The broken bodies of friend and foe were mingled in the alley, and dead enemy were found in clumps all around the area.

Rallied by their American adviser, a volunteer on his first tour in the field, the squad of Rangers fought back ferociously and to the last man. The sight of an approaching helicopter drove off the last of the enemy, leaving our man alive on the scene, the adviser himself, who was sighted in the very act of obliterating the last resistance. The after-action report made the recommendation for a medal, and Rachow added that he felt a Cross of Gallantry to be in no way excessive: he was certain that the request should be made through the Ranger unit itself.

Was it possible that he actually reached such a conclusion? On the other hand, he may have still considered himself in my debt. But it was unlikely that he would have construed the debt as large enough to decorate a murderer. Perhaps his own reputation was in some way at stake. But if it was, I could not see it. No man I had met appeared to have less concern for what people thought of him; as long as he got his way.

And the others in the helicopter. The copilot, as a quirk, had been left at the stagefield to wind up some business. The angle of approach indicated that only one gunner might have observed the scene. K.C., perhaps. Whatever Rachow asked, whatever he claimed to have seen, K.C. would certainly verify. One thing was certain: Rachow could not have simply been obtuse. His ability as an observer is unquestioned. Then again, he might have been flying with his eyes shut.

Before the ceremony he had called me to his office for congratulations. He asked if I would care to go flying with him. On a regular basis, he meant. Certainly that was an indication that he had not come to distrust me. Mooney could handle the ordinary papers, he said. He was in the process of adding a clerk to the office anyway. Actually, Mooney's function would soon be obsolete; it would be assimilated into a job of greater responsibility, which Mooney could not possibly fill. I would be required to do some night work on the more serious papers, but he assured me there would be plenty of time for diversion. And I could name my hours for coming and going. There was plenty of leverage, he assured. He pointed to the name block on his desk. Underneath his name was the title, Deputy for Plans and Operations.

All I must do is persevere, and I shall return as the town's first hero. Our other representative was not a hero, and, in any event, is no rival to consider. His background is lower class, although in our small town this is more a matter of style than of substance. Throughout his stay in Vietnam his father let the fact be known by driving a car decorated with small flags, three of them pasted on windows and one attached to the radio aerial. His rear bumper showed the red, white, and blue with the words AMERICA: LIKE IT OR LUMP IT. For my own father a single flag suffices, although, as he says, the depth of feeling is no less. In fact, it warms his heart to see the more exuberant display.

The young man got nothing but the three automatic ribbons to show off at the drive-in. And in our town, which has been overrepresented in every war, people know the difference. So, the field is open for me.

Little has changed in the office since the incident at the village adjunct. Gaudette continued happily at revisions of his plan. His wall map has been revised, as has that of the general, to include the village captured by the Rangers. Mooney says of Gaudette, *"He likes this shit!"* The truth of it is that neither of them likes it at all. Although he has been around now for a half year, Gaudette just the other day noticed the faded airborne wings above my pocket. He asked about them, adding as an afterthought that he had too much sense to jump out of planes. "You got out of it, though, I see," he said. "You're like me; you know there's no sense in putting yourself in unnecessary danger!"

149

Rachow has begun to lead Gaudette a rough life. When Gaudette turned in a preliminary version of the campaign plan, Rachow did not say a word—merely switched around the names until they were correct. A few days later he assigned another planning mission to Gaudette. The major is to draw a contingency plan for the invasion of Canada. As Rachow explained the theory, it would be quite easy to invade Canada. Pour mech units and paratroops across the central border. Strike first for Toronto, then Montreal. A classical campaign, with lots of Bismarck, Napoleon, and Stonewall Jackson. Discipline: each man flawlessly instructed as to his function and ready to die in its literal execution. Montreal would fall within the week!

War, said Rachow, has ceased to be tied down by facts. It has become metaphysical; one might say a platonic form. He asked me to picture an amphibious landing across Lake Michigan. Then imagine, he said, such things as landings by Martians; invaders from liquid planets formed of molten lava, surprised and threatened by our explorations. This is the future of military planning. War is no longer waged merely to achieve ends; it is waged as proof of its own possibility. The mortars are to be set up a certain way, for certain shot groups, in case of Martian invasions. There are reasons, listed: one, two, three, four. Certain flight patterns give maximal effect to heliborne troops in event of nuclear war; when I laughed, he showed me the manual. Possibilities entrance us. Is the pentatomic division viable? Will airboats succeed in the Delta? What troop ratio is needed in guerrilla war? Will the kill factor stay up if the troop factor is under ten to one? The navy command would like to know if naval gunfire may be successfully applied.

Gaudette demurred initially because he couldn't physically survey the area in question. Rachow informed him that more than sufficient material was available in maps and manuals and the atlas at the library. For a true professional, that is. Since that time Gaudette has been unsure how serious Rachow was. He laughs, but I have caught him in the library sitting over an atlas.

Lieutenant Colonel Nash, my rival for Lwan, has been appearing in the office daily. He wishes to inquire about my love life, he says. His tone is insinuating and overly friendly. Even Mooney does not know what to make of such behavior by a colonel; yet Nash remains a colonel, with the prerogatives of rank, and Mooney is torn with anxiety. Nash proceeds with rhetorical questions, the universal prerogative of a superior. "How's my boy today? My boy's fine I see. How is his sex life treating him? Why, the girls here call him Big Richard because they're too polite to say . . ."

It is apparent, though, that in some way he really seeks my respect. Perhaps it is because I am a link to the woman who makes his throat dry. Perhaps, too, he senses in me a rebellion to a system which has treated him badly. He is the Regional—Popular Forces adviser. A few months back, a news magazine referred to his units as Ruff-Puff. It is the vernacular of their abbreviation. He managed to get another reporter to write a story of rebuttal, asserting that the usage was actually Riff-Piff. The rebuttal has erased nothing in the mind of the general. The general swears that Nash will leave the corps with such a report that he will soon be returned to civilian life.

In some ways I suppose the army has never been Nash's tea. He salutes sloppily. His belly is soft and low like a woman's; he doesn't make the effort to pull it above his belt. Among soldiers, this is a sign of un-abashed effeminacy. Even his insinuating talk is an indication. He reveals too much. Such indiscretions do not become habits overnight.

Early one Sunday morning, as I was reading by

the pool, he appeared to disturb my solitude. He was wearing a baggy swimsuit hiked up to his chest. It was the kind of suit in which endomorphic elder statesmen are photographed at the Riviera. He had jogged the twenty yards from his room to the poolside, and I got the impression that he was out of breath. He sat in the pool chair next to mine, and undertook to strike up a conversation. He wanted to know what I was reading.

"You know, son, I'm more a civilian than most civilians."

The book was Xenophon's *March Upcountry*. It was, I told him, about a civilian who was more of a soldier than most soldiers.

Coming back after getting the award, I checked my box for mail. At least no one would be writing congratulations. Not as yet. There was a letter from E.

Someone in E.'s family has given her a sum of money with the suggestion that it be used to call me by Pacific cable. She wants me to arrange to be beside a phone at a certain time. She will reserve the cable time and we may talk for nine minutes.

I realize that I am unwilling to put her reality to the test. I have written a letter saying no. Her disembodied voice, from fourteen months and ten thousand miles, might overwhelm me. There is the plausible excuse that I am getting nearer the end of my tour and the sound of her voice might fill me with too much longing.

★ twenty-four ★

RACHOW IS MAKING GOOD on his promise to take me with him to the stagefields. Last Monday I flew with him all day. The flight down was uneventful.

While the others went for lunch, Rachow explained to me a new theorem he was working out for the defense of airfields. Airfields, he explained, were long, thin rectangles; there was no way of getting around it. The shells fired at them by Charlie had elliptical beaten zones. We knew their characteristics perfectly, because they were our own surplus from the last war. It only stood to reason, then, that there was a certain area to fire from which yielded maximum results. In fact, outside of a certain span, shelling would be ineffective. He doubted that the enemy had actually sat down to figure this out; twenty years of trial and error, however, should suffice to do what mathematics could do in the evening. The results on airfield attacks had convinced him that the enemy never deviated from the most effective firing radius. Since they carefully covered their launching area, even dumping rocket casings in spurious locales to draw us off the track, no one could be sure what the enemy practice was.

For a tactical coup, he explained, one need only input the characteristics of the weapon, the seventy-five, input the dimensions of the airfield, and perform a set of differential equations. Did I know calculus? Good. What remained was to train the defense artillery and mortars on the resultant location, and prime the helicopter strike force in daytime practice. He had reconstructed a matrix listing the probable times of the month and hours of the night for an attack. Each hour of the month had been assigned a probability.

He produced a sheaf of papers, which I read while he ate a can of C rations. I recalled K.C. saying that Rachow was forever depleting the standard load of C rations. Too busy to go for a sandwich. Rachow handed me a can of beans. His figures were accurate; his idea original and sound. I caught a small discrepancy in the arc he had drawn on the actual map, but it proved to be an approximation rather than a mistake.

"Not a bad stroke if I say so myself," he said. "I haven't decided whether to publish it, put it into effect, or merely leave it between the two of us to keep score."

We made a vertical takeoff so that rather than passing objects, we watched the ground beneath us shrink into a tabletop. The operation was going on still, not far from the stagefield. Beneath us on the right a flight of gunships were moving to a target for suppressive fire. Well behind it, to our left, was the flight of transports, full of Rangers, for an assault in case of major commitment.

"There go the condottieri," said Rachow. "You will notice that the troops are committed piecemeal, a company at a time. This is the level of tactics applied in Renaissance Italy."

I noticed only that the ground below had shrunk to a new perspective. It was difficult, without thinking of it, to distinguish trees from grass. Men, if seen at all, were only black dots. They were entirely different when seen from four thousand feet; it was as if the distance were not of space alone, but of levels of reality, as in the dream. The whole scene was nothing more than a tabletop mockup. It was perfectly clear why generals found such maps and models of value. Battles in the air have undoubtedly wrought changes in the psychology of war.

As I though about this notion, Rachow and K.C. were absorbed in a discussion of tactics. Rachow carried in his head a virtual textbook of strategy—historic battles and their contemporary application.

Nelson at Trafalgar
One cuts a column of sampans in half, outmaneuvers them, and sinks them in small groups.

Horatio at the Bridge
One assumes a position in front of enemy ground troops, who are fed onto the field of fire one at a time. One at a time they are dealt with.

Leonidas at Thermopylae Pass
It is the same as Horatio, more or less, except for its heavy dependence on favorable terrain features.

Alexander at Arbela
One launches a rapid, oblique flanking attack, in which one strafes the enemy into disarray, though unable to overpower him, then strafes him again and again before he can recover and regroup.

Stonewall at Chancellorsville
One passes over an unsuspecting column, then doubles back to assault it in a lightning thrust before a return seems possible.

A small enemy column was sighted. So well were they concealed in the growth that Rachow had to describe their distance from landmarks in fingerspans before I could see them. He flew past them nonchalantly, as if we had noticed nothing. Just beyond their field of vision, we plummeted—as if we had been hit by antiaircraft. I gripped the door handle. Circling back quickly, Rachow gave us a countdown from twenty until they would appear in flank across a treeline. On zero we moved up above the trees, and as Rachow tilted the ship to the left, K.C. fired the first burst, cutting their column in half. At the end of the run Rachow pulled sharply and swept back again, this time tilted right as the other gunner raked the middle of the line. The column was smashed at the center, hanging together only by a tendon of limp black pajamas. Rachow then circled first one group then the other until no black pajamas remained standing. I passed K.C. a piece of cloth to wipe off the oil from his machine gun bolt.

On the way back to the headquarters Rachow passed back a letter from a senior general in the states. He was being advised to give it up and come home— as soon as he could wind up his affairs.

The army had a long-standing policy of rotating assignments. It wasn't necessary to belabor for him the concept that an officer should be well rounded, developed in the many facets of a modern military team. He had really shown the utmost promise for systems work; administration as well. Even training, and technical development. West Point or no, he had friends, and there was no limitation for him. Come back. The army is not all war, you know; soldiering is not just fighting. Besides, the army is especially cautious about leaving its best timber in Vietnam. In the first place, they might be killed. In addition, it could be harmful in the long run to a man's mental stability.

★ twenty-five ★

THE LETTER was the first sign I had seen that there was pressure on Rachow. Except for the manual on "Creative Leadership," I knew very little of his career before he saved K.C. from the stockade. At the next lunch break, he was quite willing to tell me himself. He passed me a C ration dinner of ham and lima beans. When he opened his, he offered to swap me a sweet cake for the chocolate cookies that came in mine. He laughed when I refused. He shrugged and threw the sweet cake out the door.

"I've gotten to like these goddamn C's better than I like food. I even take a case every so often to my woman and have her cook them up for me. If I eat nuoc-mam I have to be corked." He took a draft of stale water from his canteen.

"The last thing I did before coming to Vietnam was to burn my dress blues. If a man is incompletely civilized, and functioning in an uncivilized profession, I can't abide a superficial effort to look like a gentleman."

He had received perfect efficiency ratings since being commissioned a second lieutenant. He doubted that any officer in the army had learned military politics faster. As a reward, he had been aide to the supreme commander in the European Theater. This job had raised him to a level with the West Pointers of his year. The work had called for the army's unique definition of administrative skill combined with the social graces. In his words, this meant clean ears, speech on cue, and a good control over the guerrilla functions of one's body.

As he talked, I got the feeling of having stayed up too long past bedtime and swallowed too much mucus. He had read about the second war—"the apotheosis of wars," as he called it—in the daily papers. He had forged a birth certificate and signed up, but had been hauled home by worried parents. The bombs on Hiroshima and Nagasaki filled him with disappointment; they had killed his war. Nevertheless, he got his commission in college. Because other fields were oversubscribed (the glamour of the moment), he had specialized in helicopters. By a stroke of luck, the Korean war had shown new uses for them and he was on the ground floor. Wounded and decorated, slightly off balance from loneliness and the war itself, he married a Japanese girl. She had proved an exemplary soldier's wife.

After the war, he had taken a tour in "systems," the new pseudo science. As far as he was concerned, its contribution was to make one ask if his immediate concern was not trivial. He answered yes and scuttled systems. Returning to helicopters, he was just in time to be a pioneer in design and tactics.

He decided that any future wars would have to be fought far within a nation's capacities, and he planned his career accordingly. It amused him that he was of Russian ancestry. He guessed right at each turn and won promotions.

Psychologically, he waited for the big war, the repeat of World War II. With it would come the requisite conditions for the role he had groomed himself to play. Then the truth hit him fully: war had come to a state of entropy! It was more and more complex, but in the process its energy was spent. If he had known sooner, he might have quit the army and written a book—on the war which had made his profession obsolete.

"How can a man hold up his head when bearing is no longer required, or even valuable. The bombs do the feats of strength; the materials the feats of fortitude. Do you know when *men* are required? When you want to do something half-assed!

"Do you know that Napoleon's generals were under thirty? The trouble with war today is that there's no way for the old men to get killed. And there's no need for genius. It's dangerous to have it."

His eyes were rimmed with red as always. Despite his look of intelligence, he had the head of a procurer. It occurred to me that D'Artagnan, failing to come off perfectly, must look like a pimp. In another age Rachow might truly have conquered a world. Or have met a world conquerer at Zama, or Stalingrad, or Marathon, and reduced his empire to dust. Then back to the farm to write memoirs and lament corruption.

Instead, he was a successful, precocious, and prematurely gray colonel who had burned his dress uniform and overstayed in a combat zone. Still, he said, it might have turned out well if the Pentagon had left off with only a few thousand men in the country. Instead it had become a testing ground, our equivalent of the Spanish Civil War. We knew, for instance, that the Thunderchief would have to be scrapped. Career men who had spent too much time on their asses could catch it all up in a quick year.

He suspected the War College. It all smacked of a simulation that had not come off. Someone couldn't get his program straightened out, and it was decided that it would be cheaper to go ahead with real men. A macrosimulation. In fact, it might be the new gradu-

159

ation exercises. He was only surprised that it was held here rather than a deserted part of Nevada. He would have expected the indigenous population to put up quite a stink. Some fine diplomacy must have taken place. Perhaps there was a stink, and it was necessary to bribe the leaders with a king's ransom. At any rate, it was an excellent training course. Not too dangerous—in spite of the scare stories, almost no one died who didn't try to—and full of little training aids to push around.

Had I heard of the Melean dialogue?

★ twenty-six ★

IT IS NO LONGER CLEAR in my memory what set off the quarrel with Mooney that particular afternoon. Some boast of mine, I suppose, because I remember him shouting,

"Will power? Will power? I'll show you about will power!"

He said he would continue our bet double-or-nothing; I didn't have will power. He tried to negotiate, begging me to bet at stakes of five dollars, truly payable. When I refused that, he had to bet gratis. He took his wristwatch off and placed it in front of me. I had five minutes, he said, to give a demonstration of will power. By five rotations of the second hand I was to will power myself into an erection. I laughed, but he was completely serious. When the time was up, he insisted on inspecting my pants.

"You see. I told you you couldn't do it. You ain't got no goddamn will power!"

"I may not have any right now," I said, "but I sure as hell have it at the appropriate time."

It was just such a statement which may have set him off.

The boy with the blocks of wood was at his usual station. The game seemed clearer this time. The stick with the tapered end was flipped into the air with the other stick acting as a sort of lever. A good toss required a quick movement with a very precise moment of force. Then, while it was in the air he tried to hit it again. The second blow was the same as that of a baseball coach hitting fungoes. This time the boy was accompanied by a friend. The new boy had a stick and a hoop, and the game seemed to require a basic skill of twirling the hoop around the stick. Perhaps the other boy had been there all along.

There was a small mud puddle in the middle of the narrow storefront. Some of the frontmost merchandise had been splashed by the afternoon rain. As far as I could tell, the goods were otherwise unchanged. Perhaps only a small item or two which did not meet the eye. It was clearly not a functioning organism, replacing inventory, meeting expenses, showing profit and loss. The old woman was living off capital like the bear in winter. She even walked slowly, I mused, to preserve what stores were left.

Lwan was waiting in her usual pose, sitting beside the little partition which shields the living quarters. The posture of relaxation, almost like that of a sleeping animal, lends itself to her pretense of a casual hello, a pretense which erupts with equal facility into argument or sexual passion once we climb the stairs. Yet she said nothing, only turned her back and led the way up the stairs.

She walked straight to the bed and sat down. I remained standing. I am not yet used to beds made of wood, not even for sitting. When they really want to be comfortable, they stack up pillows and resemble the ancient kings; I wonder why they make the beds in the first place, like American beds in every way except devoid of mattress and springs, made of wood. She pulled a pocket notebook from beneath a cushion and opened it. She stopped at the one page calendar, with little boxes for each month.

"Have the papers fini?"

"Not yet."

"When are we going?"

"At the end of my tour, unless I must extend for a few months to get the papers through."

"Oh."

She circled the data which was listed erroneously on my library card. My original date of return.

"Is this the day?"

"Yes."

"Then how can you go back to school?"

Suddenly her vehemence had burst forth and her forehead wrinkled. With her pencil she was circling another date. I saw at once that it was the date of early discharge the army had granted me.

"Of course there are still some arrangements to be made. For instance. before I met you, I had asked the army to discharge me early for school. This matter is delaying the papers. I expect an answer any day now telling me that my original tour has been restored."

"Lie."

"No, it's quite so. The army doesn't do things in a day. It's a machine, a giant bureaucracy. Do you understand 'bureaucracy'? A beehive full of stupid bees. They get in each other's way. Who told you about this date?"

"Makes no difference. Lie, lie."

"Not at all. I admit that at the beginning I was not sure. I only told you so because I wanted time to think it over. I wanted to have you while I thought about it. If I had not deceived you at first, there would have been no chance for us. You wouldn't have seen me at all. Now the papers take a little time, but I have made up my mind for sure."

"Lie. Mooney says there are no papers."

So it was Mooney.

I began to be angry. The criminal was brought to justice, but the magistrate himself had overstepped the limits. I realized how much greater than outraged innocence is outraged guilt.

Further words were useless. She wanted documents. She wanted signatures. She went so far as to demand a bondsman from the headquarters, preferably an officer, to attest to my good faith. The next time I appeared at her house I was to have papers in my hand.

On the way home I was torn between two thoughts. It occurred to me, first, that the whole matter was needless. Until I walked upstairs, it had not really occurred to me that I might test her and actually decide to marry her. As I made my defense, it seemed to me that the arguments were not entirely false. We had a good adjustment. How many marriages could boast of that? One could do a great deal worse. There was no particular impetus to marry her; I suppose that is the reason I had made no greater effort to cover my tracks. In short, there had seemed no motivation for overcoming the nuisance of actually filling out the papers. Once I was presented with the situation, in which not filling out papers was as wrought with inconvenience as the papers themselves, I had a change of heart. Other things being equal, as my father is fond of saying, I would as soon be married to her as not.

Before my mind could assemble coherent policy on this matter, the circumstance of Mooney's intervention would cut in. I had thought of myself as having at one time a very carefully drawn code of ethics. It had grown vague of late, but there was no question about Mooney's act. It fell well outside the area of fair play among men who did not like each other. It occurred to me to punish him by pure brute force. I could handle him at will, any day of the week. I would thrash him tonight in his room and leave him with a double warning; if he told, I would kill him with my hands; each time I met him in the future, I would beat him again. What recourse would he have? It was only a matter of impressing him with my utter intractability—insanity, perhaps—to make him realize that he could not report me and must skulk around in fear for the rest of his tour. Impressing him with my insanity should be simple enough.

As for Lwan, surely there was more to my feeling for her than I had acknowledged. In other circumstances, I could thank my star for not having passed her up only to realize it on the plane home. There was E. to think of, however. And the fact of my political ambitions. What locale would be sufficiently liberal to accept a candidate with a war bride? A sign of weakness, to say nothing of the interracial aspect. It was out of the question. Besides, after the requirements she had imposed, there was the matter of pride.

When I couldn't find Mooney in his room, I doubled back to the enlisted club. He was drinking with the sergeant major. In order not to miss his departure, I sat down with a table of soldiers and ordered an orange soda.

My eyes did not leave the figure of Mooney. Drinking steadily, and slowly as if he had been at it all night, he did not depart from his expression of bitterness even when laughing at the sergeant major's jokes. When he finally walked out, I was poised to intercept him, but his step was so unsteady that I knew beating him would fall outside the code.

* * *

The next day in an impetuous burst, I complained to Rachow that dissension was making my work impossible. The burden of working with Mooney was worse than having no one at all. The office wasn't big enough

165

for the two of us, and Rachow must choose and send one of us to the current opening at a border camp.

I had expected to be put in my place as a very junior subordinate grown presumptuous. At the very least, I expected Rachow to pour oil on the water, to say, "Brace up, son, his job is virtually obsolete already, and soon, when the reorganization is done, he will be returned to Saigon with thanks."

Instead, Rachow picked up the phone and asked for the personnel office. He wanted Mooney deported to a border camp without delay.

★ twenty-seven ★

MOONEY'S INITIAL RESPONSES left nothing to be desired. Yet he managed to pull himself together days before his departure. It disturbed me that even a coward's pangs of fear lacked staying power, substantially.

The day he left was the first time I had seen him in battle gear. The helmet swallowed his pea-sized head. It reminded me of the ceremonial battalions in their tunics and helmets. The suggestion of a midget recalled the paraphrase from Wilson: one should lay off enemies who are outclassed. Mooney was so thickly built, his face so constantly angry and red, that it had not struck me until that moment how absolutely tiny his cranial receptacle might be.

As he left, he insisted on shaking my hand. Rachow had not told him the reason behind his departure, but Mooney had guessed it and I felt bound to own up. He assured me that he felt no rancor, although he still profoundly hoped that I would be busted. I didn't understand the army well enough to be a sergeant. On a personal level, however, there were no hard feelings. Would I shake to that? His hand was trembling. Nevertheless, he kept a braver face than I had imagined. "I could have been . . ." he began, and trailed off.

Lwan's note asked me to meet her at home. It was

common knowledge that she had been seduced by Lieutenant Colonel Nash. He had bought her a color television set and a number of appliances. He had even looked into the question of extending his tour. It might have been necessary to write his wife: Dear, A sense of duty to my country prevents my returning home just yet. The general's look told him he had better be out of headquarters while the getting was good, so there was no longer any question of marriage.

The boy on the block was flipping his chip in the air, having become quite proficient in the year while I watched him play with it. Next year, perhaps, he would have a new toy. His friend had mastered the hoop twirling as well, and was performing certain tricks, such as holding the hoop between his legs or behind his back.

Lwan was waiting in her posture, she led me upstairs, sat down, and told me that she had been taken advantage of by Lieutenant Colonel Nash.

"Will you kill him?" she asked.

"No."

"Beat him up?"

"No."

"Why?"

"Because he is a fat man. There is no horror in harming him."

"He has harmed me."

She looked well.

"If I harmed him, my life would become a tragedy, and to no purpose. Just when things promise to go well. There is no reason to go to jail now. Whatever I do, he will go home in a month or two and his wife will spit in his face. I will think of this and you may think of it too."

She undressed in front of me, dropping her underthings with a graceful gesture, like a model. Her waist was so small I was sure I could reach around it, although of course I could not. Her breasts were tiny, perfect miniatures. She was a most desirable toy. We made love, and she asked me again about Nash. Again I refused. She pretended to be angry. We made love again and she did not ask.

"Do you know he made love like . . . a threshing machine . . . out of a CARE package!"

"No! Really?"

"Like a lawn mower."

"Really?"

"Like a tank that they do not make anymore."

"And how is that?"

"Very systematically. Up one arm and down the other. He turns the corners. Like a soldier in a parade. He is so fat he nearly breaks my bones. I was afraid I would have to stand on my head for him to be able to make any love at all."

"You will say the same of me when I am old and out of breath. Or out of ideas."

"We will never be old in the same country."

She bent forward like an infant being tickled. Then she doubled over and rolled into a tiny ball. I picked her up and rocked her.

I could visit again, she said, whenever I wished. Only call first. And for me there would be no charges.

The word of my latest heroics has reached the hometown press. Response has not been slow. My father, for one. His letter was fat and full of marginal comment, laden with complaint and exhortation. At first he must have intended a single page. In the end, I suppose he broke down. It might have been quite effective. A page, virtually blank, with a single line in the middle. He sent it anyway along with the others. Above his signature, the letter in full; *We have met the enemy, and they are ours.*

★ twenty-eight ★

A FEELING of having swallowed mucus persisted in the base of my throat. Perhaps it was a virus, I thought. I would have gone to the clinic except for a suspicion that the feeling was psychosomatic in origin. Nothing could be coughed up. If I complained of a nonexistent drip, I might be written down as a malingerer.

Perhaps all I needed was a short rest. My mind was half made up to extend my tour—to contract for an extra eight months of service in hopes of using the time to find the real action. My resolution lacked only a concession of some token sort to drag it across the line. Rachow sent me to Saigon in search of one.

On the way up I concocted the condition. The army was to agree to a thirty-day leave with a military hop to India. I had always wanted to see Calcutta, Delhi, the Taj Mahal. They were just far enough off the beaten path to give me a sense of the exotic. Tourists went there, but not as I would go. Soldiers did not go there. As soon as I arrived I went to the central personnel office and explained my proposition. The corps clerk nodded and said that by the next day he would draw up the papers. Although he pressed me to finalize my commitment, I refused categorically to sign the papers until I had a guarantee from the army on their side of it.

When I left the corps, I had been of a mind to take a night out on the town. K.C. had seen to it that I was fortified with no-sweat pills, small doses of tetracycline taken just after the action to preempt disease. He had persuaded me to use them regularly as a precaution of great aesthetic superiority.

By the time it was evening, I realized that I was not feeling up to a night out. The thing in my throat was a legitimate illness. If not, its platonic form was a reality of equal intensity in my mind. I stayed in my room.

When I woke up the next morning, my throat felt like a piece of paper with the moisture dried out of it over a heater. I was sure that it had cracked in places. My tongue was stuck to the roof of my mouth, and it too was infected with the fever. Mucus in globs had overflowed into my mouth. My tongue came unstuck with a crackling sound. Looking in the mirror, I could see it coated with a white sediment matching the visible rear portion of the throat. There were long red lesions. My first thought was of the venereal training films.

While dressing, I tried to review my situation in light of this new possibility. Several times I stopped to look again in the mirror. Each time, for some reason, I shrugged. The shrug must have been involuntary, for my mind had been put into frantic action.

If true, this would be the second stage. If only I had practiced onanism like the others—I might have noticed the tiny pimple in the initial stage. I cursed my parents for their clean-habit lectures. The second stage, I recalled, might yet be effectively treated. It would go away of its own accord, for that matter. Yet one was never sure. It is like a person's sexuality: once called into question, it remains on probational cure no matter how many demonstrations of recovered health. For this reason most states had taken it upon

171

themselves to regulate the disease: if a former syphilitic marries, he is legally bound to inform his spouse. Failure to do so invalidates the marriage.

It seemed clear right away that there was no question of informing E. She had not been raised to hear such things, nor had I prepared her for it in my letters. My course of action was clear enough. The body had let me down. I should bear up in defiance of it. It was the more reason to seek danger and its private rewards. All meaning previously inferred could be suspended. My life meant nothing: I would be free to do as I pleased. The letter I would write E. began to churn in my head.

The bus ride made me aware how feverish I had become. The other passengers seemed to be reeling around, and I barely got off at the correct street. The personnel sergeant leaned forward and said, ". . . all set. Just sign at the bottom of this paper."

The room began to wobble. I felt myself about to throw up. It's nothing, I thought. It's only my throat—it's a little sore. No, don't bother to get anyone. I'm fine.

They took me to the compound medic, and he in turn sent me to the hospital.

"What kind of no-sweat pills had I taken?" the doctor asked. I told him they were tetracycline.

"Tell your man at the black market that he was mistaken. They were penicillin. When we discharge you tonight, you will return to your hotel room. We will notify your unit of holding you over. You will report back here each morning until released."

"Do you consider it curable at this stage?"

"I should think so. Do you think I would turn you loose to die in your room? Nevertheless, you have allowed quite a culture to grow dormant while you were 'taking precautions' on your other end. Naturally, when you gave your penis a night off, and neglected the pill, it broke forth with considerable intensity. Still, we don't lose them anymore with strep throat!"

It was as if his words had cast heavy responsibilities on me. I was again responsible for a life equipped with the standard issue of complications. E. remained to be dealt with, as did Lwan. In the meantime, I looked out the window as the bus ride took me past streets where the sidewalks had disappeared under a mound of uncollected garbage. It was encroaching on the street as well, with no apparent effort being made to stem the tide.

Day after day dragged by. I telephoned Rachow and was assured that everything was under control. There would be a mound of paperwork, however, when I returned.

I sat in the hotel and ground my teeth. My thoughts were full of irrelevancies. Who built such a quaint little white hotel? What were its clientele, its economics? Did its restaurant break even on food in order to gouge out a volatile profit on liquors? I pictured French landowner, colonial lady, journalist, comprador capitalist—then the new set of rising politician, profiteer, and military attaché. Then last came the soldiers themselves. Had our army bought the hotel outright, or did it lease? Perhaps it was a loan from the latest junta, which might have taken it by eminent domain. I wondered what had become of the fancy grillwork beds replaced by army cots. Strep throat! If it is a labyrinth we traverse, it was spun by a madman without imagination. We know the worst: if there is a God, he is the property of the provincial churchgoer. He possesses no mansions but these. His kind of joke is a cracker-barrel quip at the expense of people like me—who are too big for their pants.

173

When the extent of my vacation became clear, it seemed to me that I must use the time to regroup and make decisions. Yet it was as impossible to make decisions there as on a ten-day visit to a small town. Rows of trees overhang the boulevards like crossed sabers at a military wedding. They reminded me of the oak trees in my town. Each day one says, "Business can wait a day while I sit under the trees. In a quiet spot as this, one can transact his business in a day less." Each day this is repeated until the situation is given up as hopeless. Not even generals are immune. "Just leave us alone a day," they say, "and in good time, in good time . . ." Eventually they weary of poking the people with cattle prods. In a year he will be home, but his record must be built with men who will remain when the year is up. They are in no hurry, and in good time he himself is infected. Seduced.

For no particular reason, I went ahead writing out the letter to E. which I had planned the first morning when I woke up. *Dear E., I have been overtaken by a medical catastrophe of cosmic dimension.* Only instead of saying "syphilis," I revived an old convention and substituted the words "shell shock." Otherwise I might have raised more questions than I gave answers. On the way to central personnel, my last day in Saigon, I stopped off at a military postal box; at some point the letter had gotten itself enveloped and sealed. Like the bullets in my dream, it was a messenger to a different plane of being; a real man was sending it to a puppet. Setting my cap at a jaunty angle, with a deliberate effort to be casual, as if nothing of import were taking place, I dropped it in the box.

"It's all right here. If you'll just sign . . ."
"But I don't see the guarantee of the leave to Delhi.

The flight either. In fact, it allows for only eighteen days, and that's not nearly time enough."

"Oh, that. We're very sorry, but we couldn't promise about India after all. What's the difference; all they have in India is unfamiliar germs. We've arranged for you to have eighteen days in Hawaii. White sand. Blue water. Girls in bikinis—honest-to-God American women. And if you just get a few miles off the beaten track, it'll only cost you . . ."

Although they took me to be dressed down by each superior in their chain of command, for putting them out and changing my mind, it was out of the question.

I have lost a filling. The fact was impressed upon my consciousness as the airplane took off for the corps. It was necessary to get up in the middle of the night and catch the mail plane. There were no other vacant seats all day.

The filling may be one of the recent ones. It is hard to remember them individually. Whichever, its absence was signaled by a sucking pain when I took a drag from my canteen. Such a pain can be an amazing spur to memory. When healthy, one can hardly remember the barest description of his last illness, its time, place, circumstances. When an illness is repeated, a man is thrust back to its last occurrence as though no period of health had intervened. The aircraft was flying with open tailgate. No doubt the cool air aggravated the cavity as we hovered above the Delta.

Since I had worn a full complement of battle equipment on the flight to Saigon, there seemed no need for me to return to the compound. I would merely inquire of the day's operation, where Rachow might be found, and get one of the air controllers to arrange a hitch to join him at the scene.

"If you're kidding, buddy, you're in pretty rotten taste!"

175

"No, I am quite serious. What I want to know is where Colonel Rachow is flying today and what flight might be available to get there."

"Haven't you heard? He and his crew chief——."

★ twenty-nine ★

THE DEATHS are still unreal to most of the staff. The general himself was said to be torn apart and would not appear in his office during the day. Even more unreal was the escape of the other gunner. The story he told was beginning to raise eyebrows. There would be a board of inquiry.

Rachow, K.C., and the current gunner had set out after midnight on a rescue mission. They were to see if it might be possible to evacuate wounded from a camp under siege. As it turned out, the ring of enemy troops was too tight to attempt a landing, and there was no alternative to turning back. Gunships would be available in a few hours. As the ship turned, the gunner had heard a clank. K.C. had been standing as usual in the door, expectorating and waving his private parts at the anonymous ground fire. Suddenly K.C. bend over and folded himself to the floor. Rachow had gained altitude, held the ship steady, and turned back to inspect the wound. Already there were no signs of life. The round had most likely been a fifty caliber.

Then came the part of the story generally doubted. Rachow had returned without a word to the controls and flown direct to the nearest airfield. There he had landed in the middle of the strip, and, at that point, instead of moving to the buildings, had told the gunner to get out. The gunner had been too flustered to raise a question. Before he could ask what to do, the ship had lifted off again and was rising into the darkness.

The rest of the story was a matter of evidence. The gunner had alerted the night air controller, who supposed the facts were mixed up, and that the colonel, a man whose authority was unquestionable, was pursuing his typically unusual but effective behavior. When the ship did not return within the time of its calculated fuel supply, and no other airfields had word of it, search procedures were instituted. It had been sighted by an outpost on the fringe of the U Minh Forest. Shortly after dawn a team of helicopters located the wreck, with Rachow's body. The position of the ship indicated that it had been returning from the area of deep marsh, and that ingenious efforts had failed to keep the damaged craft in the air. As for the crew chief, his body had not yet been located.

Great care is being taken in replacing the Deputy for Plans and Ops. As the general put it, his empire will probably have to be broken up. There doesn't appear to be a colonel on the horizon prepared to fill it. No one had thought of that when the position was created. Meanwhile, the general is looking for an ambitious staffer to devise a scheme for dividing up responsibility. When I heard the story, I thought of the last words of Alexander. Dying in Asia, surrounded by sycophants, he had been asked to name the one to whom he bequeathed his conquests. "To the strongest," he said. It split three ways.

My own replacement has arrived, and I have set about the job of training him. There is little to tell him, since the actual function of plans and operations seem to have disappeared. The replacement is an unfortunate case anyway, a rather fat customer from

Texas who is obliged to carry an inner tube with him wherever he goes and use it as a cushion when he sits down. He has a chronic, aggravated case of infectious boils. The very first day he called me aside for a confidential question.

"Say, you've been around for a year now and probably know the ropes pretty good. The thing is this, you see. My family back home is a long line of Indian fighters and Mexican and nigger killers—(I noticed your accent right away, buddy)—and they just ain't going to think the same of me if I come home without latching onto some kind of decorations. Maybe you can tell me what a guy has to do in this place to get his pinky into the water. I don't mean that I have to get stormed at by shot and shell or anything, but I understand that a lot of combat duty that you can get decorated for is pretty safe, and . . ."

I advised him to forget the delusions of grandeur and make a killing in the black market. If I had it to do over, I said, that's how I would go about it.

At the end of his first week, he asked me to read parts of a letter he had written to his mother. He had noticed that I was "hot on English and shit like that." Only a week or two before, a letter from a soldier, killed after the writing, had made quite a splash in the stateside papers. If his letter should make the paper, not the big dailies like the other fellow, but just his little one-horse weekly town paper, he didn't want to be embarrassed by bad grammar. He held the sheets in his hand as I read, covering certain parts which he claimed were "personal shit," but which were almost certainly lies too blatant for the eyes of a comrade. He had arrived early and knew that there were several more weeks that I would be around, long enough to put him in hot water with the other guys.

The letter was a reasonable facsimile of the published one, even to the syntax, although the spelling

179

was nothing to write home about. I record the passages which I am most nearly capable of rendering verbatim; the spelling of course corrected:

DEAR MOTHER,

I have been wanting to write and tell you what it means to be here. Nobody would choose to be here, if the decision were for him alone, but here we are, and I believe the situation calls for some explanation.

I know you would rather have me safe at home, but being here is my duty. We are fighting here for freedom and democracy. We are sacrificing, in all humility, for the principles our nation gave to the rest of the world a hundred and eighty years ago. We are struggling so that a people less experienced than ourselves in the ways of free goverment, less well equipped to stand off the tide of barbarism, may endure.

In this fundamentally sound commitment, there will be mistakes and setbacks. It is just a question of weighing these mistakes against our collective resolve.

P.S.—Don't, whatever you do, worry your dear head about your son. Just remember: I'm the one here to dodge the bullets.

It is only a matter of weeks since the disaster with Rachow and K.C., and now the headquarters must bear further bad news. Sergeant First Class Mooney, formerly of this headquarters, has become a casualty. Stumbling onto a mine while on patrol, he lost both legs above the knee. Dragged back to camp in terrible pain, he died the first night.

No one at the camp seems to have known him well

enough to go back as body escort. For that matter, the commandant has complained of the difficulty in writing to Mooney's wife, but the general assured him that good military etiquette would see him through the routine commiseration. It has been suggested, however, that escort of the body be handled through this headquarters, where he spent the majority of his tour.

The general came in person to broach the subject. He himself had heard Mooney refer to me as "his boysan." Mooney was always speaking of me. The sergeant major, in fact, remembered Mooney once saying something to the effect that I was "like a son to him." It was clear that I had been Mooney's closest friend. The general hoped that I would think of this duty as a privilege. My tour was nearly up anyway, more so than anyone else on the staff. The army would probably discharge me at its nearest base. This way the headquarters would lose a minimum of manpower days. Think about it, he said.

The boy with the wood chip had apparently graduated. He was nowhere to be seen. Lwan led me upstairs with heavy steps. She herself has been emotional lately, crying easily, and quite unpredictably, like a loose-handled bucket sloshing over on your pants.

Sitting on her bed, I tried to sort out the truth about Mooney. A spurious curmudgeon? A man of gruff exterior? My well-being held secretly in his heart? And I—the son he could never have? Fantastic, genetically and socially impossible! For no reason, I began listing his acts: the hat, the threat, the bet, the comeuppance with Lwan. A son indeed! A front for office pride is more like it. He was the *old-army* type. Whatever dissension went on, the sergeant major must not know. Paste it over in public. Should I mourn him for this?

What if he *had* seen it in a movie: Gruff Old Man with Heart of Gold? What was it but a diversion to a still insufficiently hardened conscience, a conscience that perhaps rebuked him for power-mad abuse of subordinates. He had gotten his. That was that.

"Mooney's dead," I said absently to Lwan. As she looked up with wide and lonely eyes, I wondered if it were possible. Possible that behind her myth of using me she had loved me all along. Possible that behind my myth of using her, I had loved her as well. Possible that Mooney, in the very act of abusing me, was in his deepest self so lonely that a contrapuntal truth reared its head and shouted to the world that I was like his son? For the third time in this war, I felt a lump in my throat.

The general's clerk came that evening to tell me the matter was taken care of. Another soldier had broken his arm. Useless as a typist, he was escorting the body home. I would stay until the end. After all, I alone knew the combination of the safe.

★ thirty ★

YESTERDAY I saw a dentist again. He asked me to let him put in a temporary, since the oxide he prefers is out of stock. By all means, I said.

He noted from my chart that the army has performed extensive repair work in my mouth. As I was outprocessing, he felt it timely to inform me that the service bore responsibility for each tooth it had worked on. The adjacent ones also. This benefit applies for the rest of the patient's life. I thanked him for this information and tossed off the quip that in that case the army was pretty well on the spot with regard to my whole mouth.

This morning when I got up I looked at my skin in the mirror of my hotel room. It struck me that I had been too preoccupied with other business to get down to the task of developing a tan. My face, of course, is burned to an oily brown. It is quite striking on my craggy features, set against sunbleached hair and the blue of my eyes. Yet I had wanted so to unveil a brown chest when performing the seduction ceremony. The girls at grad school will have to settle for musculature and the myth of the combat hero. I could, of course, use my week of vacation to cultivate a tan, and maintain it through the winter with a lamp. A trip to the islands would do the trick. But that is no different from what the jelly-butts do. It probably wouldn't match my face at all.

When it came time last week to book myself to Saigon, I realized that I had developed a peculiar aversion to flying. In order to duck it, I got myself put on a motor convoy. It had nothing to do with fear. I suppose I have come to feel like the passenger on Lufthansa: given the flight data by a meticulous captain, stuffed with sausage and other delectables, propped on pillows by girls with sensual, lupine faces and hairy arms, and told that every effort is being and will be made for my comfort. *As long as I follow orders.*

My convoy was ambushed, but I was unable to take advantage of this final opportunity to smell powder and observe the gift of death. I was busy with a personal problem: it was my luck to remember a chaplain who gave a talk called "No Atheists in Foxholes." Thinking of him, I huddled in the bottom of a ditch, pressing with every fiber of my being not to pray, not even subconsciously. Not even my fingers were allowed to cross. A grenade rolled into the mud at my feet. I could have stood on it, saving the others and becoming a legitimate hero. Instead I picked it up and chucked it back.

After all hopes were abandoned, a flight of F5Fs appeared as saviors. My hands were still clenched in determination to die an apostate. Only then did I notice that the next man had received a round between the eyes. The mask part of his face was hardly damaged, but upon picking him up I saw that the bullet had flattened out and pretty well cleaned the content through the other side.

How incongruous it is that I am writing of such things. For myself, only my books have suffered. They were caught in a torrent before I could get my window drawn. Each of them is full of mildew and loose pages. Wet books make me sneeze.

I am telling of my experiences as they seemed to me. Later I shall go back and read between the lines. Although it will probably do no good. If I am truly an intellectual, the truth will not be in me.

An intellectual is the measure of nothing. He triumphs. What of it? He escapes. So what? If everyone were able to escape, the world would be in anarchy. He is extricated from the rules. It is by wit; he is a fluke. A dinner-table bore. His answer to everything is prowess, prowess, and more prowess.

Is it humility or arrogance that makes one feel unrepresentative? Or should I say "arrogance or humility"? Does the order make a difference? If I say the former, one would suppose that I had always perceived it to be humility, only to have come now to suspect that it may be arrogance. While on the other hand . . . Or is it the other way around?

It will be good to see M. again, to have a drink with him. The Irish devil of a revolutionary! At times I had come to fear that he might be only a straw man. Imagine! A figment drawn up inside my head. Soon I will be watching him crush beer cans.

The personnel sergeant in Saigon was bent on giving me a medal for my action with the convoy. One of the survivors, from a distance, had observed my behavior. My spunk in getting rid of the grenade. He may even have thought it one of ours, which I was aiming at the enemy.

"But I didn't stand on it. I only threw it back."

"Oh, that's been taken into account," said the sergeant. "Nevertheless, you're due a Bronze. Throwing it back is almost as good."

"No," I said more firmly. "I already have the medals I want."

185

"Oh, it won't detain you. We'll just copy down the information and mail it afterward to your address. So there's no worry."

Still I refused. His eyebrows came together.

"Are you sure there wasn't something in that incident that didn't meet the eye?"

"Of course not,'" I said quickly. "If you're set on giving me another medal, send it to this address."

I gave my father's number. Although I shall not be there the names are the same. The old man, worse luck, didn't even manage a citation in his war.

It had been said that we would have another chance to reenlist. From the looks of it that station was by-passed. Perhaps we went by it and I didn't even notice. So now I must plot a course of action to be put into effect upon return.

There is redemption through art. I could do water colors like the combat artists. The public loves it: big, burly Marines and their poignant stylized scenes of mother and child in the battle zone. But I'm not ready for that. Men who draw pictures must at bottom realize that for their function to exist, other men have to lead dreary, ordinary lives and need the relief of things to see. Yet down deep one suspects that artists never feel quite the same about a person when they learn that his life is not devoted to brush and canvas.

Then there is politics, which keeps cropping up. After the second war, a veteran ran for office on the slogan "Congress Needs a Tail Gunner." I could use that, or a variation. The man was successful and went on to an enormously rewarding career in calling his enemies unpatriotic. All the same he struck me as primitive in method. With my intelligence, I have no doubts that I could avoid his mistakes.

At least it can be said that my liberal convictions persevered through the whole muck. It has, however, struck me what a fine maneuver it would be to base a whole career on the conservative line, then switch just at the decisive moment. In the meantime, since the point of view of the "right" is stupid and vulgar, and the majority of people are likewise, one could enjoy interim successes.

Back at school, in my dorm, there was a Coke machine that was perpetually robbing everyone. Sometimes it returned the dime. Sometimes a nickel, but no Coke. Sometimes it kept everything, even a quarter, and hummed in your face. We all swore to write letters to the company or petition the school authorities. One night after it had robbed umpteen victims, I saw a little guy come up to it and lose his last dime. After swearing for several minutes, he took a couple of paces back, made a running jump, and kicked it squarely in the middle of the door. For a moment it rumbled, like a man hit in the gut with brass knucks. Then it gasped and burped forth a Coke and two dimes. The boy, who didn't live in our dorm, opened the Coke, pocketed the dimes and drew back to kick again. Again it rumbled and belched. When I came down in the morning, a repairman had opened the door with a crowbar and was puttering around with a forlorn look. Warm Cokes with their tops off were lined up in ranks four rows deep in the hall.

The buses have stopped, and the men from the first shuttle are outside and milling around. An officer is lining them up in ranks, shouting at them. They are waiting. The lines are going inside a depot shack to turn in their issue of tropical equipment. It seems to be taking an inordinately long time, and I do not yet see anyone emerging from the other side. To be fair, though, this herding seems to be the only way to get it done. There is a queuing function—it makes up a test problem in every course of applied calculus —which tells exactly how many attendants to employ and exactly how long each individual should have to wait in order to reach maximum overall efficiency. These fellows have probably done the computation with reasonable accuracy. Now my bus is about to unload.

We are back again. I had to pay for two pieces of equipment. They were deducted from the pay I have coming for unused leave. I had not wanted the equipment in the first place, but everyone must draw it. I dropped mine out the tailgate of the plane that took me down to the Delta.

The din on the bus is growing. The man to my left is coloring the final square on his calendar. I wonder if he will start a new one in the states to count away the anatomy of his lifetime. The idea must have occurred to many of them. If so, I wonder upon what part of the anatomy these lives will converge. The officers in the seat ahead are discussing syphilis. One of them had a terrible scare,

". . . the shit out of me my yin-yang would rot off!"

My life is trying to flash by as if I were falling off a building, but there is no time. They are about to herd us out of the buses again. There is no time to stop for a question. We deal in answers, not questions. As our leader said in his last appearance. You want to deal in questions, get your ass over to Europe where history played out a century ago. Questions are for people who can't get a hard-on.

In the crowd from the last bus is a former aide to the Commander, U.S. Forces; I saw him save his chief from being photographed in front of an air conditioner. He is returning a hero, eventually to be a general himself. While a company commander, he

188

called in napalm on his own position. To save face, the army gave him the Medal of Honor.

It is raining, and tropically cold, shivery. Malarial cold. For forty consecutive weeks I have refused to take my primachoroquine, or is it chloroprimaquine? and nothing has come of it. Instead I get strep throat. It is raining in sheets. The power of suggestion is so strong that I am afraid I may wet my pants. It's like standing outside the theater, the movie over, and no one there to pick you up.

We have boarded the plane. Sometimes an airplane can be a great relief. The facts below begin to dwindle into perspective. Distance reduces them to stage props. I will see green, brown, and blue. There will be roofs, trees and grass, and strips, perhaps rivers.

The destination is San Francisco. When Odysseus came home, the gods made him carry an oar over his shoulder, inland, until he reached a place where the population had never seen the sea, nor oars, nor tasted salt. M. is likely to claim that I am charged with just such a special and messianic mission. He will seize upon the superficial impression of disillusionment. For my penance, there will be a levy of radical fervor. It is unclear what to say to him, unless that I am, by constitution, a soldier.

The stewardess is serving drinks. The returnees are laughing and shouting. They seem drunk already. They are vying to give the stewardess a pinch. A major is getting out of his seat, lunging across the aisle. They would all like to . . .

The others have noticed, through the starboard windows, a peasant plowing with a water buffalo. They are shouting at him even though he can't hear a word. Goodby, you mother . . . Oh, well. I suppose the girls on this flight are used to it. Hard cases, no doubt, they know what they are in for. There's extra pay in it, at least. The guy on my left, a shrimp of a lieutenant with postadolescent acne, is reading over my shoulder. Now he has stopped and is blushing. The officers in front are holding up glasses for a toast.

Down the runway and into the night. It will be a clinical phenomenon. Two days in one. We are beginning the shortest day. In five hours, sunrise to sunset, there will be splendid colors, oranges and purples. The vets will comment from time to time, taking out scratch pads and making little globes with their hands. I will be compelled to watch them all the way to San Francisco.

BOOKS • ABOUT
VIETNAM
FROM AVON

DISPATCHES
Michael Herr   58255-4 $2.95
"What a passionate, compassionate, brilliant book this is. With
uncanny precision it summons up the very essence of that war—its
space diction, its surreal psychology, its bitter humor—the dope,
the dexedrine, the body bags, the rot, all of it." *Chicago Tribune*
"The best book I have ever read on men and war in our time." John
le Carre

THE BIG V
William Pelfrey   67074-7 $2.95
An excellent novel...Mr. Pelfrey, who spent a year as an infantry-
man in Vietnam, recreates that experience with an intimacy that
makes the difference." *The New York Times Book Review*
"THE BIG V is courageous." *Washington Post Book World*

WAR GAMES
James Park Sloan   67835-7 $3.50
"In WAR GAMES the reader is confronted with the gut issues not
only of the war in Vietnam, but of war and militarism in general...
tautly constructed...may become the new Catch 22." *Library
Journal*
"WAR GAMES is studded with gems." *Saturday Review*

AMERICAN BOYS
Steven Phillip Smith   67934-5 $3.50
"A disturbing, moving and significant novel, not just about war but
about the men and boys who fight and die in them." *Milwaukee
Journal*
"The best novel I've come across on the war in Vietnam." Norman
Mailer
